Twisted

FATE

emery jacobs

Editing & Formatting: Rogena Mitchell-Jones, RMJ Manuscript Service, LLC
Proofreading: Terrie Meerschaert, Indie Editing Services
Cover Design: Amy Queau, QDesigns
Front Cover Model: Drew Truckle
Photographer: Eric Battershell Photography
Back Cover Model: Rainy Wilson
Photographer: Mandy Hollis Photography

DISCLAIMER: Due to sexual situations and language, this book is intended for readers 18 and over.

Table of Contents

For the only person who has the ability to deal with me on a daily basis and still love me. Thank you for your support and encouragement—because without it, I would never accomplish anything.

Losing our way,
searching vainly for more,
vanity makes us ebb outward,
until our love drifts ashore.

~Alex Maxwell, 2016

PROLOGUE

SEVEN YEARS EARLIER

JACK

MY HANDS ARE trembling as I slowly lower the handle to open the door to Kappa Sig's biggest party of the semester. I stumble over the threshold and maneuver my way through the crowd of drunks in search of Piper's long blonde hair. Unfortunately, I think every girl here may be blonde. And then I see her. Maddie Foster. Piper's best friend and a complete fucking bitch. I move toward her until I'm close enough to grab her wrist. She spins around—takes one look at my face and her smile immediately fades.

"Where is she, Maddie?"

"Where is who, Jack?" She smirks.

I squeeze my eyes shut and silently count to ten. I do this to keep from knocking that smart-ass look off her face. I know she's a chick, and I would never hit her, but she's made it her mission over the last year to piss me off every chance she gets.

"So are you meditating now… in hopes of envisioning her exact location?" She laughs.

I clench my teeth as I pull her in closer. "I'm not in the mood to play games with you tonight. Tell me where Piper is."

"What makes you think I know? I am not her keeper." She rolls her eyes and pulls her wrist from my grip.

"I know she's here. So take your damn phone out and send her a warning. Let her know the bullshit ends tonight!"

1

"Wow, Jack. I didn't know you had it in you to be so possessive. I have to say I'm more than impressed. Maybe even a little turned on." She winks and then leans over toward the girl standing next to her. They both laugh. She takes a couple of steps toward the crowd, and I watch her hand move toward her back pocket. She pulls out her phone, and then I know. I know Piper is here with *him*.

She's quickly lost in the crowd, so I return my focus on finding my girlfriend. Looking over my shoulder, I notice the staircase I've been avoiding since walking through the front door—because up those stairs is the last place I want to find her. I drag my hand through my hair and take a deep breath. I put one foot in front of the other as I make myself trudge up each step. When I reach the top, I turn slightly to see Maddie standing at the bottom peering up at me. Her eyes are dark and she's moving her head from side to side. Ignoring her plea, my eyes return to the empty hallway in front of me. Shuffling slowly, I stop in front of each door. Leaning in, I bring my ear close to listen for voices. One room, two rooms, three rooms and nothing. My heart rate increases with each stop I make. When I reach the last door on the right, I hear a voice. *Her voice. Piper.*

Even though I knew what I might find tonight, I'm still not prepared to hear her moaning behind the closed door. I take a deep breath before placing my hand on the knob. Turning it slightly to the right, I push open the door. My body freezes as heat rises to my face. The image in front of me will be forever imprinted in my mind. Piper's naked body is straddling some guy, and she's rocking her hips back and forth. Her body quivers just before she throws her head back and screams his name.

"Caleb!"

Mother. Fucking. Caleb. And I lose it.

CHAPTER 1

JOVIE

MY EYES FLUTTER open, and I roll over to escape the blinding sunlight seeping through the window shades. I stare at the bright red blinking numbers before I make a quick scan of the room. Black dresser, cluttered night stand, beige lamp, hunter green walls… a body lying next to me.

Shit. This is not my bed, not my room.

I jolt up and swing my legs over the side of the bed. I must have fallen asleep.

Crap. Now it's daylight, and I know my dad's awake. If he looks in my room before he leaves for work, I'm so freaking busted.

"Jovie, what the hell are you doing?" I glance over my shoulder at Liam's messy brown hair and questioning gray eyes.

"What does it look like I'm doing? I'm leaving. It's six o'clock in the morning. Can't believe you let me fall asleep here last night."

"I guess my farewell fuck was a bit much, uh? Too tired to crawl out of bed and hurry home like a good little girl."

He wraps his arms around my waist as he pulls me into his warm naked body. Any other time, the warmth of his skin and hardness of his body would be a welcoming feeling.

But not now. Not today.

3

I have too much shit swirling through my mind. And right now, it's all about me getting through my bedroom window without getting caught.

"Wanna go for round... five or is it six?" He chuckles.

"No. Let go of me." I grab his hands and pry his fingers apart.

"Look, Liam, I'm serious. I've got to go. Please, just let me leave."

Over the past year, Liam has been my dedicated booty call, but last night was the final page of the book of this so-called relationship. Today, I'm heading out of this Podunk town that I've called home for the last seven years. Brownsboro, Georgia. No thanks. This depressing little town of twelve-hundred poor souls will never be graced with my presence again.

"Fine. Get dressed—I'll take you home." He rolls over, gets out of bed, and grabs his jeans off the floor.

"No, you can't. My dad usually leaves for work at this time. What if he sees us? I can't chance it."

I have to get the hell out of here before I have a complete meltdown. After jumping out of bed, and throwing on my shorts and t-shirt, I tread into the adjoining bathroom. One look in the mirror says it all. Knotted hair with a whole lot of frizz paired with smudged mascara and a— "Liam!"

"What's the problem now?" he steps behind me and our eyes meet in the mirror.

"Is this a hickey on my neck?" With a shaky hand, I point to the red mark just below my earlobe.

"Damn, Jovie. You need to chill. You're nineteen and leaving for college in about four hours. So, if you get caught... big fucking deal. Does it really matter? What are your parents gonna do? Absolutely. Nothing. And no, that's not a hickey."

He licks his finger and runs it across my neck removing the red—lipstick. I'm such an idiot. I turn to face him, placing my hands on his cheeks. He covers my hands with his as he pulls me

4

in for a quick kiss on the forehead.

I take a deep breath and look into his gray eyes before saying, "Does it matter? Yes, it matters very much. My parents think I'm perfect. That's the only reason they're allowing me to go to school twelve hours away. If they realize I'm not, then they may not let me go. And that's not an option."

"I hate to shatter your beliefs, my little rule breaker, but your parents know you're not entirely perfect. No one is. It is unrealistic to even go there. Because it does nothing but cause this." He nods his head toward me, indicating my current state of disarray. "You scream—nervous breakdown—and I don't want that for you. I know why you're leaving and I understand. But I hope being away from this town and your parents is really all that you expect it to be."

"Wow, Liam. What a great inspirational before you go speech. Now I feel all warm and fuzzy inside. Seriously, I appreciate you trying to talk me out of falling apart, but really, I'm good. No more meltdowns for this girl."

I wrap my arms around his neck pulling him in for a hug. He means well and I'm gonna miss him, but we both knew this day was coming. And neither of us is heartbroken. We've had so much fun. Spending time with him has made me a better person. He's a great guy. Just not my forever guy.

He pulls back from the hug and looks into my eyes before he rewards me with a sly grin.

"Let's get you home so you can get your car loaded up. I know you're ready to get on the road to your future."

"Thanks. You're the best."

"Is it that obvious?"

He wraps his arm around my waist leading us out of the bedroom toward the front door.

As Liam inches his truck toward my driveway, I stretch my neck out the window to look for my dad's police cruiser. Being the Police Chief's daughter doesn't make my life any easier. And I know Liam is quite fearful of my dad. Considering he is the youngest officer the Brownsboro Police Department has on its force. He faces my dad daily—with our little secret. So bringing me home in broad daylight is an honorable move on his part. Because my dad wouldn't hesitate to slap on the cuffs, throw him in the back of his car, and haul him off to jail.

"He's already gone. So you can stop at the end of the driveway."

He pumps the brakes gently until his truck comes to a complete stop. I lean over and press my mouth to his. His tongue moves along the seam of my lips wanting more. I open my mouth slightly to take one last piece of him. His tongue caresses mine gently before he moves his hands behind my head and pulls me closer. The kiss is flawless. It's the good and the bad of the last year rolled into one heartfelt moment. He lets out a deep moan, and I know I have to stop before this gets out of hand. I pull my lips from his and stare into his eyes.

"We can't," I whisper.

"I know, but it doesn't mean I don't want to," he waggles his eyebrows.

Damn, this boy is all kinds of cute and sexy. He'll have another late-night booty call lined up before I make it to the interstate.

"I'm leaving now. Remember, we promised no long goodbyes. It's not necessary. You're an amazing guy with entirely too much to offer. I'm a tormented soul clawing her way to independence. And we will find our happy place. Just not together." I smile.

I'm not worried about my decision because somehow, I know everything is going to be okay.

I grab the door handle just as I hear him say, "See you around, Jovie."

I glance over my shoulder to get one last look at my past.

"Yeah, see ya around, Liam."

Climbing out of the truck, I turn toward my house and say a silent prayer that my mom is still asleep. I quickly make my way toward my bedroom window.

My lips curl into a smile, and for the very first time in what seems like forever, I'm truly happy. Because in a few short hours, I will be free from my parents, from this town, and from the memories of the reason we ended up in this shithole in the first place.

CHAPTER 2

JOVIE

LEAVING MIGHT BE more difficult than I initially thought. My mom is leaning against the back door with tears flowing freely, and my dad hasn't even bothered to show up for good-byes.

"Stop," my best friend Layla says.

"Stop what?"

"Feeling guilty, having second thoughts—you know, all that shit that's going on in here." She pats the top of my head with her hand.

Layla has been my best friend since the day I moved to Brownsboro. When I arrived in this shitty little town, I had no one. My mom had decided to coil up into a shell and not let anyone in. My dad immersed himself in his new job. And me, well, I was so lost from reality because I had been yanked from the only life I'd ever known. There was no one to guide me and give me what I needed to survive.

Layla found me that first day... sitting on a bench in the park across the street from my house. My head hung low and tears were streaming down my face. Most twelve-year-old girls would have been embarrassed, but I was too consumed with sadness to care. She offered me her friendship that day, and I accepted it like a starving man who was offered a single slice of bread. I craved her kindness, and that's what she gave me. I was grateful then and even more so now. We were both just kids at the time, but she was there. Always there. And that's what I needed.

"I'm fine, really. I just need to get out of here. This is too damn depressing. It's almost as if I've been thrown back in time to the day we left Houston to move here. All the fucking crying from my mom and my dad being... well... unavailable."

Layla grabs my last suitcase and shoves it into the trunk of my car. There's no room left for anything but our two bodies in the front seat. When I decided to go to school twelve hours away at the University of Houston, Layla was right there with me. I think secretly she'd wanted to leave Brownsboro too, but she couldn't admit it until I convinced her to come along. Her parents have been so supportive of her decision and helped both of us in this little dream of mine. Her mom took us to Houston last month to tour the campus, find an apartment, and a job. Lucky for us, her mom has a good friend who owns a sports bar and grill. So, that's where we will be working. My life is coming together. Or I guess I could say full circle. I'm going back to the place where it began.

"Yeah, but that's not the case. Today you're going back to the place you love so much. And I get to go with you!" she squeals.

"Hey, you. Gonna give your mom a hug?"

My mom approaches me with a freshly washed face and not a tear in sight. God, she's really trying. I lean into her as she wraps her arms around my waist. I return the hug trying to be careful not to squeeze her frail body too hard.

"Please be safe. Don't make your father and me regret our decision to let you go," she says.

I take a deep breath and ponder how I should respond. I want to tell her it's not their decision to make, and I would have gone without their blessing. But I don't because I want to leave on good terms with my parents.

"I promise to be safe, Mom." She nods and gives me her famous half smile.

"Your dad isn't going to be able to make it. There was an

emergency so he had to go out on a call." An emergency in this town. Right.

"I need to see him, Mom. I have to tell him good-bye. Call him. Please." Holy Crap. Why am I freaking out? *Calm down, Jovie.*

"What if something happens, and I never get to tell him good-bye?"

My heart rate picks up as my chest tightens. A second later, my entire body is tingling. *It's only panic. Take a deep breath.* Nothing will happen to him or me. Damn. I hate the idea of losing control, but the panic comes from nowhere. It creeps up and grabs hold of my body. But I refuse to take medication like my mom just so I can keep my shit together.

"Jovie, sweetheart, your dad isn't avoiding saying good-bye. There's a fire down at the old Flea Market. He had no choice but to go."

She squeezes my hand as if I'm her lifeline. I stare into her eyes and force a smile. A sudden calmness comes over me. And I know the panic is subsiding. That's the way it goes. It grabs a hold, shakes the shit out of me, and then it's gone. Never know when it's coming, but at least, I have some security knowing it always leaves. At least for a while.

The panic attacks started a couple of months after we moved from Houston. My parents took me to counseling for a while. It helped a lot. Eventually, I learned to control it so it no longer controlled me. But over the last six months, it has come back with a vengeance. The return of my anxiety attacks is a sign that it's time for me to go. To find my way in this world, make my own decisions, and leave the security of my parent's sheltered world.

"I know he's busy. I'm really sorry I freaked out, but I'm okay now. And we really need to get on the road. Layla's parents are supposed to meet us at the interstate, and I don't want them to have to wait." Her parents didn't want her to be without a car, so they decided to follow us to Houston and then fly back.

"You ready, friend?" Layla's voice pulls me away from my thoughts.

My mom releases my hand before leaning in and kissing my cheek. Still no tears. I'm proud of her.

"Are you kidding? I've *been* ready." I step away from my mom moving closer toward my car.

"I love you, Mom. Please tell Dad the same."

"Love you, too. Call me when you stop for the night."

"Will do." She walks toward the house without another word.

We climb into the front seat of my car and latch our seatbelts. I shove my key in the ignition and turn it right. My car roars to life—ready to take me far away from here.

But not before Layla clears her throat and asks, "How long have they been back?"

I knew the questions were coming, but I'm not ready to go there. Not today. Today is the happiest day of my life. I'll avoid the questions, and when that's no longer an option—I'll lie.

"Who?"

"It's no who, Jovie. Don't play dumb. You know exactly what I'm talking about." Her voice is both stern and soothing.

"The anxiety isn't back. Okay? What you witnessed is the first attack I've had in years. I think it's kind of normal to have anxiety about going to college and making your own way. Don't you?" I grip the steering wheel a little tighter as I throw the gearshift in reverse.

"Yeah. Whatever, Jovie. But I'll be watching you, and if this panic thing is anything like it was when we were kids, you're getting help. I'm not gonna just stand by and watch my best friend relive her past. Remember, no yesterdays. Only tomorrows—full of parties, boys, and firsts."

"Firsts?"

"Yeah. Our list, or should I say, your list because we both know my life has been a little less sheltered than yours has. So my list is neither as long nor as important as yours."

"The list." I smile.

Layla continues, "I think I'm more excited about the list than you are... I can hardly wait for your first party, first drunken night, first public make out session, and for you to get that tattoo you're always talking about."

"We have plenty of time for all of that. Plus, I bet there are a lot of firsts that my sheltered ass doesn't even know exist."

"You're right about that." She giggles.

Hopefully, we have left the subject of my returning panic attacks. I'll just have to be really careful not to let her see me have another one. I pull away from my house, and my eyes stay focused on what's ahead of me.

"Houston bound!" I let out a scream as we head toward the interstate.

CHAPTER 3

Eight Years Earlier

Jack

"IN CLOSING, I will leave you with this thought—remember each and every one of you will eventually learn to accept the reality of your loss and work through the pain and grief. It may take some a little longer on this journey, but I promise, it will get better with time."

Annie reaches for my hand and wraps her fingers around mine. I give her a gentle squeeze as I lower my head. I hate this for her. A grief support group is not somewhere you want to find yourself at nineteen years old. It would be hard enough to lose one parent, but to lose both in one instant is the absolute worst.

"If anybody needs a minute or two alone with me—for questions—I'll be here. And for the rest of you, I'll see you next week."

Annie leans over and whispers, "I'm gonna stay and talk to Sally for a while. You can go. Bennett's gonna pick me up in twenty minutes."

"Are you sure? Because I'll wait until he gets here. I don't want you to be alone."

"Jack, look around. There are people everywhere. I'm not alone. I love you and am so thankful you came here with me tonight, but I'm okay. I promise." Her gaze moves around the room. She's looking for Sally, the grief counselor who leads the group. Sally has become an important person in her life over the last few weeks. I'm glad she has someone to talk to because the reality is I suck at this shit. Even though Annie's my best friend, and has been since I can remember, it doesn't mean I can hash out this death thing with her. I'm not built for that kind of conversation, but it doesn't mean I don't listen to her when she needs me. I just don't know what to say or how to act. Plus she has Bennett. They have been dating for a few months, and he seems to be a lot more sensitive to all of the emotional shit. At least, more than I am. So I'm glad she has him, too. I still love her… We're family, and I will always do whatever is needed to help her through this difficult time in her life.

I release her hand, and we both stand. She wraps her arms around my waist giving me a hug. Then she buries her face into my neck as she mumbles, "You go. I'll see you tomorrow."

"If you change your mind, text me and I'll come back." She releases her hold from around my waist and nods. I smile, knowing she doesn't have the strength to return it, but hey, she needs all the encouragement I can give her.

I turn and head for the door. As I step out of the room, I notice there are dozens of people spilling out into the hallway. St. Luke's United Methodist Church is a Thursday night hangout for a lot of people. It's a place for those dealing with loss and addictions to be a part of their own support group. I think it's great that the church opens its doors for all of these torn souls searching for some normalcy in their life. I can only hope that Annie finds hers.

Rounding the corner, I see a flash of blonde hair just before I'm pressed against the wall by a small firm body.

"Just go with it. I'll explain later." I nod looking into her pleading blue eyes. She lifts the corners of her mouth with a genuine smile.

"Piper, what the hell?" The voice is echoing from down the hall. It's loud and male, so this is probably going to end badly.

I push gently against her small body, trying to break free.

The last thing I want is to be trapped against a wall when some guy starts swinging. She presses her body into mine as if she's letting me know she's not budging and that I'm not leaving.

"Look—Piper—you need to step back so I can leave before your boyfriend makes it over here. I—" Before another sound leaves my mouth, her lips press against mine. She pulls my bottom lip between her teeth and tugs. I'm so fucking weak. This guy's about to beat the shit out of me, and I suddenly don't care. Initially, the kiss is distant, cold, and reserved, but in an instant, her mouth becomes aggressive and needy like it's the last kiss she'll ever give. Her body trembles as her hands find my face. She suddenly pulls away and takes a step back. We both watch the short dark haired guy exit the building.

"Not willing to fight for you?" I ask.

"He has no reason to… he's not my boyfriend. Just some guy who bugs the shit out of me every week."

"Every week?"

"Yeah, every week because I'm… well… I come here for the meeting. It's for my mom. She's an alcoholic, so I come to these Al-Anon meetings to help me learn to cope."

"So that guy you were trying to get away from is here every week harassing you?"

"I know. It's quite annoying. Thank you for playing along and for the kiss. It was, well—nice."

"Nice?" I laugh. "You make it a habit of kissing random guys in church hallways?"

"Normally, no, but I made an exception just for you." She moves in closer. "You wanna do it again…?

She pushes her body against mine as her hands slide up the front of my t-shirt to the bare skin of my neck.

"I take your silence as a yes," she says before crashing her lips into mine. Moving my hands to her long blonde hair, I pull her closer. Nearer. Until there is no space between us. My tongue meets hers, and I forget where I am. I forget that the only thing I know about this chick is her name and the fact that her lips feel so good pressed against mine.

She pulls back staring into my eyes. Blue. That's all I can focus on until she laughs. Her laugh is as beautiful as her eyes.

She places her hands on my shoulders, pulling herself up to my ear. Then she whispers, "Umm…" before placing a wet kiss on my cheek. Her tongue traces a trail back to my ear and she repeats, "Umm… I really want to get out of here—with you, but your name. I have to know your name."

Rapid breathing, along with my inability to focus on anything she says, causes me to forget for a split second where we are. We need to leave now before I do something that should never be done in the hallway of a church.

"Your name," she whispers.

"Jack." She has me so distracted I can barely remember my own name.

"Jack, please take me somewhere. So we can finish this." She moves her hand to my dick and tugs.

"Not here," I say as I moan.

"My thoughts exactly." She grabs my arm and we race out the door.

CHAPTER 4

JOVIE

"YOU WANNA GO to a party tonight?" Naomi asks.

I look over my shoulder and find her leaning against the bar. Her hazel eyes staring back at me. Naomi is one of the few friends I've made since moving to Houston a little over a month ago. We work together along with Layla here at Overtime, a sports bar.

"What time? I don't get off until eight."

"I'm not going until about nine-thirty. Oh, and Aubree's going, too. So it will be the three of us." Aubree is one of Naomi's friends from childhood. She has a three-year-old daughter, so I bet she probably doesn't get out much. At least, they invited me to the party and didn't ask me to babysit.

"Okay. I'll go." Naomi looks down her narrow nose at me. "What? I said I wanted to go."

"Shit, girl. I heard what you said, but you sure didn't sound like you meant it. If you don't want to go, it's no biggie. Just thinking you don't go out much for a college gal. You know, drunken keg parties, hot guys, and one-night stands. Does it ring a bell?" No, actually, it doesn't. I've been so busy with school and work that I haven't even thought about going out. And Layla, she's already had a handful of dates, so she's been too wrapped

17

up in her own life to worry about mine.

"Yes. I really want to go to this party with you, Naomi. Please... take me to the party with you and Aubree."

She laughs. "Good. Let's get this shift done and get the hell out of here."

* * * * *

I park my car directly behind Aubree's black SUV. The house sitting in front of me is enormous. Three stories of windows. No curtains. No shades. No blinds. Open for the world to see the hundreds of people drinking, dancing, talking and laughing. *Who the hell lives here?*

A rap on my window pulls me away from my thoughts, so I look to my left. Naomi. She's standing beside my car peering in with her perfectly sculpted raised eyebrows.

"Are you getting out or what?"

"Yeah, give me a second." I take a deep breath before opening the door and stumbling out. Shit. I shouldn't have worn these damn heels. But they look so good with my fitted lace crimson blouse and black shorts. At least, that's what Layla said before she made me wear them.

"You'll be fine, Jovie, we won't leave you alone. I promise," Aubree says as she throws her arm over my shoulder—almost pulling me down to the concrete sidewalk. She reeks of alcohol and can barely walk without swaying. Grabbing her arm, I sling it off my shoulder and steady myself so I don't tumble to the ground. No wonder Naomi's their designated driver tonight. Because Aubree is in no shape to be driving. Hell, she's really not in any shape to be walking.

This is all new to me. I've never been around anyone drunk before. I'm not judging. It's just different—weird to see someone purposely do this to herself. No control. Dependent on others for their safety. I can't go there—because I know all too well what happens to people who drink too much. They cause death. And then my life goes to shit, and I'm moved halfway across the country to start over.

"Are you coming in?" Naomi's dull eyes and firm lips tell me that she is irritated with me or maybe it's not me. It's probably Aubree and her drunken state that is causing the irritation.

I step over the doorsill and am immediately swallowed whole by the crowd. Within seconds, I've lost both Naomi and Aubree. So I wander through the mass of people looking for a familiar face but knowing I won't find one.

This house is incredible. At least, the part I can see. The floors are dark hardwood with rugs scattered throughout. The walls are so white it looks as though they are scrubbed daily. There isn't much furniture. A couple of black leather couches facing a huge flatscreen TV mounted on the wall. And a bar situated in the far right corner. I continue to move away from the crowd toward the back of the room when I notice more windows. Wow. Whoever lives here really likes to be seen. As I approach the back windows, I notice the water. A lot of water—a lake. It's hard to believe anyone would just open up their home to all of these people. I continue to stare out the window at all the beauty. The plump moon hangs low in the sky and gives just enough light for me to see the dark waves as they spill over the sand. This place is amazing.

A loose grip wraps around my arm, and I turn around to see Naomi without Aubree. I hope she's okay. She doesn't need to be alone in her condition with all of these people.

"Where's Aubree?"

"She's fine. Passed out in a bedroom upstairs with the door shut and locked. Ya know, to keep all the perverts out."

"Good. I was kind of worried about her. She had a lot to drink?"

"Not too much, but for her, it was plenty because she doesn't drink very often."

"Hey, gorgeous. Glad you could make it." A blond-haired

guy approaches Naomi. He leans in placing a kiss on her cheek.

"Stone. I've been looking for you." She returns the kiss before saying, "I locked Aubree in the yellow bedroom upstairs. She is wasted." He nods and mouths 'okay.' Like it's not a big deal.

Must be his house. He's young and gorgeous. Probably late twenties. He has shaggy blond hair with crystal blue eyes—strong jaw line. When he smiles, a small dimple appears on his right cheek. But what I appreciate the most about this blond beauty are the tribal tattoos that decorate his right arm. I want to inspect them a little more, but I don't because getting caught gawking at some guy I just met is not happening tonight.

I hear my name and realize Naomi introduced me to this Stone guy. I greet him with a simple smile.

"So, Jovie, Stone owns Southern Stain—you know the tattoo parlor I've been telling you about." Naomi clears her throat before she continues. "Jovie is interested in getting a tattoo, and I've been telling her about how good you guys are. I think I've convinced her to come by. Right?" She looks at Stone and then at me. I nod giving her the answer she wants.

"Cool. Here's my card with the hours and location." Stone reaches into his pocket, pulls out a few business cards, and hands me one. I take it from him and notice my hand is wavering slightly. Shit. I quickly stuff the card in the front pocket of my shorts. I listen to Stone and Naomi talking but have no idea if I'm included in the conversation. Right now, all I can focus on is my breathing. It's rapid. *God, please don't let me hyperventilate.* The tingling starts at my fingers and moves up my arm until a twitch takes over my right eye. I have to get away before I fall apart in this room full of people. Why is this happening here? I haven't had a panic attack the entire time I've been in Houston. I thought it was over. But obviously, it's not. Maybe it's because of all the people, or the unfamiliarity of this house. Alone. The need to be alone overwhelms me. Naomi doesn't know about my panic attacks. And I don't want to introduce her to my mental health issues tonight.

"The bathroom, where is it?" I interrupt their conversation, but at this point, I really don't give a shit. I need to go, to run, and get away from all of these people. So I can breathe or at least, fall apart alone.

"Down the hall past the staircase. Second door on the left. Are you okay, Jovie? You don't look so good," she says.

"I'm fine. Just need the restroom." I force a smile, but I know it's a failed attempt. I rush down the hall to find the bathroom, and luckily, the door is open. I push through and slam it shut, locking it before I slide to the ground.

I lower my head between my knees and wrap my arms around my legs. Deep breath. "One. Two. Three." Deep breath. "Four. Five. Six," I chant. "I'm all right. I can do this. It's just a damn party, for Christ's sake," I whisper. My eyes are heavy with tears, but I refuse to release them. I will not cry.

"Hey, are you all right?" a deep, raspy voice asks.

What the hell? Am I hallucinating? Just great. I go from anxiety and panic to hearing voices. I know the door was open and the room was empty when I walked in.

"Do I need to go get somebody for you?" the same voice asking another question.

I tilt my head back and rest it against the door. My vision fuzzy due to the unshed tears, but I see *him*... towering over me like some kind of tattooed Greek God. He tilts his head to the right and his eyebrows furrow. My eyes regain their focus and my vision of *him* becomes much clearer.

Short brown hair that spikes just slightly in the front. His eyes are a rich golden brown—like whiskey. Narrow nose with a chiseled jaw line and full lips. He has just enough scruff to know he probably hasn't shaved in three or four days. And he's wearing a fitted white t-shirt that doesn't leave much guessing for what he's got going on underneath. Tattoos. And a lot of them, along with a broad chest and the biggest arms I've ever seen.

I pull my lip in between my teeth and bite down. My face is hot from embarrassment, but my anxiety has vanished. I place my hands on each side of my body to push myself up so I can get the hell out this occupied bathroom and away from this gorgeous guy standing just inches in front of me. Strong hands grip my waist, and he lifts me to my feet in one swift movement. I look away, praying he is going to walk out of here and end our little encounter.

"Did something happen? Did somebody hurt you? Are you sure you're okay?" He's spewing questions faster than I can wrap my mind around them. I refuse to tell a stranger why I would lock myself in a bathroom and then proceed to freak out.

Completely ignoring his question—I stare into his brown eyes before asking, "Have you been in here the entire time?"

"Yes."

"Where?"

"The bathroom is in the back corner. This section up here is just a lounge or some shit like that."

This is just great. My first experience with an extremely hot guy plays out like this. Ugh!

He doesn't move, and his brown eyes remain focused on my blue ones. His breath is slow, even, and warm on my cheek. I drop my gaze to his mouth. And those full lips of his form a perfect lop-sided grin. Holy shit, he's sexy.

I reach behind me and grip the doorknob, wanting like hell to get away from this forever-lasting moment of humiliation. Before I can search for the lock, he moves in closer, his body demanding me to stop what I'm doing and shift my eyes back to his. As if I've completely lost all self-control, I give him what he wants. My stare moves from watching his beautiful mouth to gazing into his golden brown eyes. He tilts his head and leans in.

Oh. My. God. I think he's going to kiss me. Is it okay to kiss a complete stranger? *Yes. No.* I look away with hopes he will release me from his spell.

But his hand immediately finds my cheek and brings my gaze back to his before he says, "Don't do that."

"Do what?" I whisper.

"Look away. Your eyes. Do I know you? How do you know Stone? Who are you here with?"

Why does he do this? Never just one question but multiples. How can I answer him when I can't even remember the first one, much less the two or three that follow?

"No, you don't know me," because, trust me, I would never forget a guy who looks like a God.

Bang. Bang. Bang.

I flinch, not immediately realizing someone is pounding on the door directly behind my head. He drops his hand from my face, pulls his eyes from mine, and reaches around me to unlock the door. I take a couple of steps sideways to move out of his way so he can open the door. Then he walks past me—out of the room without saying another word.

CHAPTER 5

JACK

I PUSH THE door open entering Southern Stain, Houston's premier tattoo parlor. The cool air punches me in the face as it does every day. It's a subtle reminder that I'm still alive—doing what I am supposed to do. Art. On the greatest canvas of all…the human body.

The lobby is empty so I head down the hall toward my station to check my schedule. It's Thursday, which equals the late shift for me. Not a bad gig considering Thursday night is ladies night at Jake's, which is the bar next door. There are always at least half dozen hotties staggering in looking for a little attention. And that brings a smile to my face.

As I unlock the door to my station, the chime alerts me that someone is up front. I shove my keys in my pocket and make my way back to the lobby. I'm still wearing my smile in hopes of greeting my first client of the day, but that is quickly shot to shit when I see the tall blonde standing near the counter. After taking one good look at her pleading brown eyes, I was wishing like hell I'd thought twice before taking her home from the bar three weeks ago.

"Halle, what are you doing here?"

Nothing pisses me off more than for a hook up to try to manipulate her way into my life. I never bring anyone here because this place is my sanctuary. The only place I'm truly content. Southern Stain is my home, my livelihood, the place I function at my best. I don't need some random chick that I've

24

been fucking to show up here to tarnish it. But it never fails. Every. Damn. Time. I should know better, but I don't. So, here I stand in the lobby once again with a chick I've fucked a handful of times staring at me. The gleam in her big brown eyes has faded, and I sense she's about to shed a thousand tears. *Please don't cry. At least not here. Take that shit to your car.*

"I wanted to stop by to say hi, and I was also just wondering why you left. You were gone when I woke up this morning."

"I'm always gone. You know I never stay all night. And you also know that I don't want you showing up here—this is where I work." I have made a colossal mistake with this chick. And now's the time to fix it. It's gone on far too long, and with her showing up here today is all the proof I need. Cutting her loose and accepting my punishment is where this conversation is headed.

"I've just been thinking about how much we've been together over the past few weeks, and I'm kind of hoping you would change your mind about those silly rules you have."

"We've been hooking up for three weeks, Halle—three." I hold up three fingers so she's not confused. "And it doesn't matter if it were six weeks or six years. My rules don't change. I think we went over this the first night. I don't spend the night. And I don't do whatever this is you think we're doing. You have apparently mistaken our fucking for more than what it is."

I'm such a dick, but sometimes I have to be to end something that I should've never let happen in the first place. I don't blame myself because I'm honest from the first night. Whether or not she listens and understands is completely up to her. I don't spend the night. I don't do any kind of relationship period. An occasional text for a potential hook up, but no daily texting. No hanging out at my place. And absolutely no showing up at Southern Stain. She knows the rules, but she has chosen not to follow them.

"What are you saying, Jack?"

"I'm saying you need to leave. This thing we had is over. It was over the minute you showed up and questioned me about our non-relationship. I'm not mad. I'm just done."

"You know what? Fuck you. The sex isn't even that great anyway. Or at least, it's not for me." She takes two steps toward me, and before I can grasp what is actually going down, my cheek takes the wrath of her open hand. What the hell? Sweet fucking Halle just slapped the shit out of me. I've seen Stone slapped by plenty of pissed off women but never have I been hit in the face by a small open hand. And damn, my cheek is burning and my jaw is tight. It hurt. She turns on her heels and storms out the front door.

"That was fucking great. I just wish I had walked up sooner so I could have witnessed the entire conversation and not just the hit." I look over my shoulder to find Annie leaning against the wall smiling.

"Yeah, well, you didn't miss much. The slap was the best part of the conversation."

"I just finished up with Taylor when I heard your voice. I let him leave out of the side door because I didn't want him to walk in on whatever you had going on. Figured it was—what's her name again?"

"Halle, and no, you don't know her. She was a mistake. She wasn't able to handle the no relationship part of our fucking. You know how you women are." Annie laughs and walks back down the hall.

"Absolutely, all women are crazy. Fucking every night doesn't equal a relationship. I don't know what the hell she was thinking." Her voice fades away as she enters her station and closes the door.

Rubbing my jaw, I head back down the hallway. The chime goes off again before I reach my destination. Now I'm pissed. It's one thing to slap me and leave, but don't come back for a repeat or to apologize because it's not happening.

I trudge back toward the lobby, and as I round the corner, I say, "Look, Halle, I'm not in the mood for…"

Fuck. Me. It's not Halle. Not even close. It's freak-out girl from Stone's party last week. She's standing in the lobby looking directly at me. Fucking beautiful. Long black wavy hair with porcelain skin. Big full lips that are painted pink today, instead of the deep red from last week. And those eyes. So. Damn. Familiar. To the point of making me a little uncomfortable—which rarely ever happens. I shouldn't stare, but I can't look away.

"Hi. I guess you were expecting someone else?" she asks.

"What?"

"Halle. You thought I was some girl named Halle, right?"

"No. She just left and I thought it was her coming back, but it's not—it's you." The girl with those haunting blue eyes… that I've thought about a hundred times over the last week.

"Yeah, it's just me, Jovie." Her mouth twists with uncertainty.

"Nice to meet you, Jovie. I'm Jack."

"You work here?"

"Yes. What brings you in today? Maybe a tattoo or piercing?" She doesn't appear to have any recollection of me or our time together in Stone's bathroom—or maybe she does but doesn't want to relive it. And I'm good with that.

"I'm thinking about a tattoo, but now that I know you guys do piercings too, I've decided that's what I want." She folds the small piece of paper in half that she'd been holding and tucks it in her bag. I assume that's her tattoo design, but I'm not gonna pry. At least not yet.

"Let me get the paperwork for you to fill out, and we'll get you that piercing." I walk over to the counter and grab a clipboard and a pen. When I turn around, she is fidgeting with the strap on her purse. She's nervous. Then why is she here? Most people walk in this place knowing and ready. They don't even want to do the paperwork. But not this chick. She's either very unsure of her decision or scared as shit. I only hope she doesn't have another moment that has any resemblance to our last encounter.

I decide to lighten the mood a little so I ask, "Where do you want the piercing? Eyebrow, belly button, nipple, or…" I look below her waist, so she knows exactly what I'm asking. She takes the clipboard from me without saying a word. Her cheeks become a bright shade of red and her lips quiver. Shit. Maybe I made things worse, but at least I gave her something to think about.

A few seconds pass before lifts her head and looks directly at me.

"So, Jack, I'm actually considering having my nipples pierced. What do you think?" her face is overtaken by a smirk that's cute as hell.

Didn't expect that. Not. At. All. Thoughts of her without a shirt on immediately run through my mind. I'm a professional. Gorgeous half-naked women don't affect me, at least not at work. I do this every day.

So, with a straight face, I take in a deep breath before saying, "That sounds great.

"I do actually have a question," she says as she hands me her completed form.

"What?"

"Is there someone else here? That works here, of course. Like a female who could possibly do my piercing?"

What the hell? She's screwing around with me. Nice move.

"Yeah, Annie's here. I'll check with her to see if she has time to take care of you today." I turn and walk away—hoping like hell she doesn't see the disappointment on my face. Fuck. My. Life.

CHAPTER 6

JOVIE

THIS GUY THINKS he's so damn cool. He's handsome, arrogant, and I assume, an asshole judging from the hand print on his cheek. But for some strange reason, I find him attractive. Not just attractive, but really, *really* beautiful. He's probably trouble, but what do I know about trouble? Considering I'm nineteen years old and have been sheltered from the real world my entire life. And now the first hot guy who comes along and triggers my girlie parts to go crazy has to be the same guy who saw me fall apart last week. I can only hope he doesn't remember me.

"Hi. I'm Annie. Jack told me you were interested in having your nipples pierced." I look toward the counter to find a petite girl with long black hair smiling at me. Damn. I guess I made quite the impression. Jack didn't even bother to introduce me to this Annie person.

"Hi, I'm Jovie. Nice to meet you. No, I'm not interested in having my nipples pierced. My belly button is what I decided on."

"But I thought Jack said you were interested in having your—"

"I did tell him my nipples, but I changed my mind." I smile convincingly.

"Okay, then your belly button it is. Follow me, and we'll get started."

* * * * *

29

Less than fifteen minutes later, she's done. No pain and no blood. Annie helps me stand, and I walk over to the mirror. It's beautiful. A silver star in the center with smaller stars hanging from each side. It's a perfect size. I love it. She goes over all of the instructions for cleaning to avoid infection.

"No swimming for four-six months or until it's healed completely. A shower is better than a bath. Try not to sleep on your stomach. No tight fitting clothes to that area. Blah, blah, blah." I hear nothing. I'm still amazed I did it. I realize it's not the tattoo I wanted, but that will come later. This is my first real accomplishment of proving I can do what I want in the real world without my parent's guidance. And without having a panic attack. This is definitely a proud moment for me.

"What do you think?" Annie asks.

"It's so beautiful. Thank you!"

"I'm glad you like it. You're right. It's beautiful."

I continue to stare at my new piercing while Annie cleans her station.

"So, Jovie, what do you do? Work? Go to school?"

"Both. I work at Overtime. You know the sports bar. It's actually not far from here. My friend, Naomi, told me about you guys, and I met Stone the other night."

"So, you've met our fearless leader?"

"Yeah, but we were only introduced. I didn't stay at the party for long. But he seems nice."

Annie lets out a chuckle. "Nice? Stone? I guess he can be. School... you said both. Where are you in school?"

"The University of Houston. My best friend, Layla, and I moved here from Brownsboro, Georgia about a month ago to go to school. So far, it's been great. Just still trying to get adjusted, you know?"

"I do, but having your best friend with you probably makes the adjustment period a whole lot easier. At least you're not all alone." She looks over at me and then smiles before she goes back to cleaning.

She's right about that. I don't know what I'd do without Layla. Even though we don't spend a lot of time together, at least she's here with me. A deep cough pulls me away from my thoughts as I look toward the open door leading to the hall. Jack. I quickly pull my shirt down over my exposed stomach. How long has he been leaning in the doorway? I bet that sneaky bastard watched the whole time. I should have asked Annie to close the door.

"Annie, your next client is here," he says never making eye contact with me.

"Sure. We're finishing up. Tell Lottie I'll be with her shortly." He nods then pushes off the wall and walks away.

"No questions?" Annie asks.

"Nope, I'm good. Thanks again."

"Sure. Maybe I'll see you around sometime. If you decide on a matching tattoo, just stop by and I'll be happy to take care of you."

I pay her and throw my purse over my shoulder. I head out of her work area toward the front of the store. When I reach the lobby, I do a quick scan of the room. No Jack. Damn. He must be busy. I didn't need to see him again, anyway. I raise my top and take one last peek at my accomplishment for the day and smile before pushing open the door and walking toward my car.

CHAPTER 7

Seven Years and Nine Months Earlier

Jack

"OH, JACK, IT'S beautiful. And it didn't even hurt. You're the best boyfriend!"

Piper stands in front of the mirror and checks out her new piercing. The small silver flower sits on her belly button with a blue stone placed precisely in the center. Every single thing about her is perfect.

I can't believe she's mine.

Fucking luck or maybe fate.

I thank Annie every day for taking me to that meeting three months ago.

"The stone matches your eyes," I say.

"I didn't notice, but it does. Thank you."

She lowers her shirt and slowly looks up. Her blue eyes meet mine and darken with desire. Her gaze travels to the door of my station.

"Closed and locked," I mumble as I grab her wrist pulling her body in close to mine. Her lips find my neck and then my face. Her mouth moves quickly as she scatters kisses along my jawline until she reaches my ear.

"I need you to fuck me, Jack. Now. Against the wall."

The sexual tension starts the second she lies down on my

table for her piercing. My hands on her skin. The sexy way she moved her hips every time I touched her stomach. Piper is one of the most sexual chicks I've ever been around. It's as if she can't help herself. She can be completely satisfied one minute and tearing my clothes off the next.

I slam her against the wall. Her lips meet mine and it's on. Hard and fast just the way she wants it. No foreplay, just fucking. She grabs the hem of my shirt and tugs on it until it's lying on the floor. Before I get my pants down, she is completely naked.

"Fuck me now, Jack. I'm ready. I just need you inside of me."

"A condom. I have to get a condom," I pant.

The sound of tearing foil pulls me away from my search. She's got it open and reaching for my dick within seconds.

Her fingers thread through my hair as our lips collide. I lift her, trying to avoid too much friction against the new piercing, but it's pointless. Her legs wrap around my waist, and I slam into her. She writhes and grinds until she finds her release and then frees her legs from around my waist. Sliding to the floor, first licking and kissing my chest and then my stomach, until she reaches her destination.

Quickly, she rolls the condom off and slides her warm mouth over my erection. She licks from the base to the tip and then wraps her lips around it and gives a hard pull. I move my hands to her hair and guide her mouth down my shaft until I feel resistance. The back of her throat.

Damn, this is un-fucking-believable.

"Fuck, Piper. I don't think I'm gonna be able to last..."

I try to push her away, but she's not going anywhere. I explode in her mouth and she swallows every drop. I fall to the floor beside her. She climbs onto my lap and kisses me. Long and slow. A smile tugs at her lips as she pulls away.

"God, I love the way you taste," she mumbles while giving me one last peck on the cheek. She stands and dresses quickly, and then pulls her long, thick blonde hair into a ponytail.

"You're beautiful, Piper."

"You're not so bad yourself, Mr. Alexander, but you need to get up and put on your clothes unless you plan on sitting on the floor naked for the rest of the night."

I stand, grab my clothes, and dress. She blows me a kiss goodbye before she hurries out the door.

CHAPTER 8

PRESENT DAY

JACK

ONE MONTH. THAT'S exactly how long it's been since I've seen those beautiful blue eyes. And now they're staring back at me while I struggle to spit out my order. Jovie Blake. If someone told me she worked here at Overtime, I would've insisted we go somewhere else.

"Just bring me a beer, whatever you have on tap." I look at my buddy Fish across the table and he nods in agreement.

"Make that two."

"Are you guys ready to order or do you need a couple of minutes." She glances at Fish and then back to me. Shit, the sooner we order, the fewer times I have to watch her walk up to the table wearing half a shirt with shorts that barely cover her—well, I assume her ass, but I haven't watched her walk away yet. Fuck.

"I'm ready. A cheeseburger and fries. No onion. And he'll have the same. Right?" I look at Fish.

"Yeah, sounds good."

"Two cheeseburgers and fries," she repeats.

"And the beer. Don't forget the beer," Fish says.

She smiles and turns to walk away. My eyes travel from her red Chucks up her toned legs and stop at her—yep, her ass—there it is peeking out of those fucking shorts.

"What the hell, man?" Fish looks at Jovie walking away and then back at me.

"What?"

"I mean, first, I can order for myself. And second, why were you in such a hurry to get rid of a hot chick?"

"I'm not. I mean, I wasn't trying to get rid of her. I'm starving." He raises a brow and looks down his nose at me. He doesn't believe a word I just said. Colton Fisher, or Fish as most everyone knows him, is not only my coworker at Southern Stain, but he's also a friend. He's been around me long enough to know when I'm full of shit. And this is definitely a 'full of shit' moment.

"How many paintings do I need to bring to display for the showing?"

"Way to change the subject, but I'm not buying," he says.

"I'm not changing the subject. We came here to talk about the gallery crawl, so that's what I'm doing."

"What's up with the waitress? You fucked her, and now you're shitting yourself because you have to face her. Am I right?"

He couldn't be more wrong. I'm avoiding her because I don't want to fuck her. I'm crazy as shit. I want to fuck her, but I can't do it. Looking into those eyes while I was inside of her would break me…again.

"No, I didn't fuck her. I met her at Stone's party a couple of months ago. Then she came into the shop a week or so later, and Annie did her piercing. I don't even know her. And *you* need to pull your head out of your ass and remember that Brandy would remove your balls if she knew you were looking at another chick."

Brandy is Fish's on again, off again girlfriend. They've been doing this relationship thing for about eight years. She keeps a tighter rein on him now because the last time they were off, he knocked up a one-night stand and now has a three-year-old daughter named Gemma.

36

"All I'm saying is she's hot. And I've never seen you look the other way."

"Well, take notice. This is me looking the other way. She's not my type. Can we please change the subject now?" He knows me too well. But for now, I'm done. I refuse to discuss Jovie with him anymore.

"Sure, man. Whatever you want. I just don't know why you're being so damn sensitive about some chick."

"I'm not. Subject change, remember?"

"Okay. What the fuck ever. About the gallery crawl…I want to display ten of your paintings. They need to be similar. All have the same theme. No fucked up bullshit—I only want what's real. This showing will give you the jump start you need in the local art market or it will destroy you."

"I know, and I appreciate you giving me this chance, man. It means a lot to me. I love the shop and my customers, but I need this. I need to show the world my paintings."

Every year toward the middle of November, the downtown art district has a Gallery Crawl. Each of the six galleries come together for one night to display work by undiscovered artists in the Houston area.

Fish is lucky enough to be gallery number six. He inherited a warehouse on the edge of the art district three years ago. He transformed the upstairs into a two-bedroom apartment, complete with a studio. And the downstairs is a gallery displaying his art. This is the second year he'll be part of the Gallery Crawl. And I'm pretty damn excited he chose to introduce my paintings into this exclusive world of artists and collectors.

"Here's your beer, guys. Food will be out in a few minutes." She smiles at me, then spins around, and walks away. I will not stare at her ass. I refuse. My eyes remain focused on Fish and the fucking smirk he's wearing.

"Just fucking look," he mumbles.

"Ten paintings. Sounds easy enough. I'll come by the shop in a week or two, and we can look through what I have." No, I didn't look. I remain focused on the task in front of me. Turning up the chilled mug of beer, I take a much-deserved drink.

"Since you're refusing to discuss our waitress, tell me about your latest fuck buddy or hook up. You know whatever you kids are calling it these days. I've been out of the scene for so long, I feel like an old man at twenty-seven."

"You have Brandy and Gemma. You have a family, so a hook up is the last thing you need to hear about."

"Wait a minute, man. I'm not married to Brandy—I don't even live with her. She has her own place across town. I love my daughter, but I don't even know her mother, remember? Met her at that concert you forced me to go to, and then got so drunk, I fucked her in a bathroom stall. Ring any bells. I still blame you, asshole."

"Very funny. You control your own dick. I told you to stay away from her. Said she looked like trouble. And I was right. Of course, I love Gemma, but damn, the hell that woman put you through when she was pregnant. And then Brandy. You just need to keep it in your pants, bro."

"Hey there! Here are your burgers and fries. Do you need any refills?"

"No, we're good for now, Naomi. Thanks," I look from Fish to our waitress. It's Naomi, one of Stone's regulars. What the hell?

"Where's our waitress?" Damn, I know that sounded rude, but I need to know. For my own selfish reasons.

"Jovie?" I nod and keep my focus on Naomi and not Fish's laughter.

"She wasn't feeling well, so I told her to go home. We're not that busy. And she looked like she was going to puke."

Shit. I hope she's not having another one of those episodes because I don't think she would be in any shape to drive. Maybe I need to go out front and see if she's still here. Then I could maybe drive her home. No. What am I thinking? Drive her? What a fucking joke. I don't drive anyone but myself.

"Do you think she was okay to drive?"

"Her roommate, Layla, picked her up."

"Do you know her, Jack? I mean outside of here?" Naomi asks.

"Yeah, I was kind of wondering the same thing," Fish says as he throws his head back in laughter.

"No, I mean, I met her at Stone's party a few weeks ago. She said she was there with some friends. Then she came in the shop, but Annie took care of her. So again, no, I don't know her."

"She was at Stone's party with Aubree and me that night. She didn't mention meeting anyone. But she only stayed about thirty minutes. Now that you mention it, she wasn't feeling well that night either. Umm… I hope whatever she has, isn't contagious." Naomi shrugs and walks away.

"Not a fucking word." I glare across the table at my friend.

"Look, man—I understand your reasons, but it's been a long time. At some point, you have to let the past stay in the past. What happened that night was fucked up, but it wasn't your fault. Let it go and just live."

"Am I breathing? Am I walking and talking? Yes, yes, and yes. So I am fucking alive. I don't need you or anybody else to tell me about my past or remind me how messed up I am. This is my life, and I choose how I live it. And if you or Annie or whoever the hell else doesn't like it, then you all can go fuck yourselves. I'm done with this conversation and this meeting." I stand—stepping away from the table, and I feel Naomi's eyes on me. I glance over at her, and she quickly looks away. Turning toward the door, I walk away, never looking back at my friend.

CHAPTER 9

JOVIE

"AT WHAT AGE did your panic attacks begin?" I try not to roll my eyes at Dr. Jane D. Birch PhD., Clinical Psychologist. I really wanted to see a counselor, not a psychologist. But according to my mom, Dr. Birch is the only 'crazy doctor' on our insurance in the Houston area. If I want to see a counselor, I have to fork out the hundred dollars an hour myself. And that's not happening. I'm here visiting with the kind doctor because of the last anxiety attack I had two days ago. It was so severe I had to leave work. Not to mention Jack was there, and I didn't want him to see me in that panicked state *again*.

"Around twelve, I think. They started just a couple of months after my family moved to Georgia." I hate being here. The fact that I have no control over my own emotions sucks. No fucking control. It's ridiculous to think after doing so well all those years and now, *boom*, I'm back to square one.

"Where were you living before you moved to Georgia?"

"Here." I glance around the room taking in all the drab gray walls and dark furniture. It's really conducive to making someone feel better about his or her shitty life. Good thing I'm not depressed.

"Here, as in Houston?"

"Yes, Houston."

"Why did your family move to—?"

"Brownsboro, Georgia," I answer while she shuffles through her papers looking for the ending to her question. This is the worst part of letting someone in. I have to tell my story. The

40

story I dislike more than any panic attack. The story that was never mentioned when I was growing up. The reason my life is a mess at this very moment. But I chose to come here. I'm asking for help so that I can move on with my life. Go to school and work like a typical nineteen-year-old. And not live in fear of when will be the next time I'm huddled against the wall talking myself out of a panic attack.

"That's right. Brownsboro, Georgia. Now, why did your family move from Houston to Brownsboro?"

I take a deep breath and exhale slowly. Tears pool in my eyes, but I'm able to keep them from falling. At least for now. It's been so long since I've talked about this. About her. I close my eyes and squeeze them tight as a tear rolls down my right cheek. I have to do this. I need to be better.

"We moved because of my sister."

"Your sister?" Dr. Birch raises her eyebrows and adjusts her square framed glasses on her small pug nose.

"Yes. My sister died when I was twelve, so my parents thought it was a good idea to move me twelve hours from the only home I'd ever known."

"Tell me more about your sister's death." Of course, she wants more information about the one thing that's going to break me. Tears fall freely now as I picture her lying on that deathbed at the funeral home. She was beautiful. It's times like now that I wish she hadn't been taken from me. She would have known how to fix me. How to make the anxiety go away. She would lie in the bed with me at night and tell me stories about how exciting college life was. She had tons of friends and always had at least ten guys vying for her attention.

"She was so young. Only nineteen. She left to go out one night and never came home. The next time I saw her, she was dead. I don't know what else to say." My breathing is heavy and there's not a chance in hell that the tears will stop anytime soon. Dr. Birch hands me a box of tissues, and I quickly grab one and cover my face.

"I know this is difficult for you, Jovie, but your mind and emotions are in overload. You are having these panic attacks because, even though you don't realize it, you're experiencing the loss of your older sister…again. You're nineteen and living in the same city that she had lived in. And I bet she attended the University of Houston, too."

"Yeah, she did, but what does that have to do with anything?"

"Why did you choose to come back to Houston, Jovie? Why not somewhere else? There are colleges everywhere. Why here?"

"Because this is my home. This is where I lived the first twelve years of my life. I just wanted to come home."

"I don't believe you. This is not your home. Brownsboro, Georgia is your home. You are here because you are looking for something, and I believe it has to do with your sister."

Okay. Now she is really pissing me off. I'm not paying her to be a bitch. I'm paying her to help me get better, not to make me want to punch her in the face. Because that's what I'm feeling right now. She is so far from wrong in her assumption. I grab another tissue and blow my nose because tears streaming down my face are one thing, but snot pouring out of my nose is something entirely different.

"You are wrong, Dr. Birch. I'm here for me. I have chosen my path in life, and it begins here—in Houston."

"You are here for closure. You have never really recovered from the death of your sister. And I bet your parents sheltered you, controlled your every move, and never let you talk about her. Am I correct?"

Ugh. This bitch is getting under my skin. I may just chance it with the anxiety and panic because the only thing she is going to accomplish is adding anger to my already existing emotional disarray.

"Yes, my parents sheltered me. And no one was allowed to

talk about her. But the closure bullshit. I'm not buying it. I loved my sister with all of my heart. I do believe the combination of her death and my parents uprooting my life is the reason for my panic and anxiety at age twelve. But not now."

"I understand today's meeting may have been a little overwhelming for our initial visit, but I truly believe your anxiety will get better. And I am here to help you. Think about the things we discussed today, and we'll pick up where we left off next week. If you need me before then, don't hesitate to call."

I want to tell her that calling is the last thing I'll do. I really don't want to make this a weekly habit after today's meeting. But I promised myself I would do this for at least a couple of months. It beats seeing a psychiatrist and being medicated.

"Okay. See you next week." I stand and move toward the door.

"Jovie." Stopping, I turn and look over my shoulder at Dr. Birch.

"Yeah?"

"You're going to be fine. I promise. Just don't give up."

"I know. And I won't. I'm not a quitter." I walk out of her office and into the hallway. Finally, I'm able to breathe. This has to work. I have to get better. I refuse to let anxiety control my life.

CHAPTER 10

JOVIE

I STAND OUTSIDE Jake's Bar waiting on Layla. I hope she arrives soon because, to be honest, this place is pretty creepy after dark. Coming here tonight is her idea. She's dating the guitar player in the band, Nocturnal Revolution, and they play here twice a month. Naomi's going to stop by a little later, and truthfully, a night out with the girls is what I need. I've been super busy with midterms, work, and my secret meetings with Dr. Birch, so I haven't had time to hang out with my friends and relax.

The wind picks up, and pellets of rain strike my face. I step under the awning in front of the bar to keep dry. I need to go inside before the wind and rain make a mess of my hair. I spent over an hour straightening this unruly chaos on my head, and just five minutes of this weather will have it frizzy and out of control. *Hurry up, Layla.*

The sound of footsteps followed by a loud thud and then laughter in the alley between Southern Stain and Jake's pulls me away from my thoughts. It's probably not safe to take a peek, not in this neighborhood, but my curiosity has gotten the best of me. Ignoring the wind and rain, I step down off the sidewalk and stretch my neck around the side of the building to get a look at who's causing the commotion. The lights in the parking lot give off just enough of a glow that I can see Jack standing on the bottom step that leads to a side entrance to the bar. He's holding onto a girl who is standing a step above and is trying playfully, to

44

push him away.

"I have to go. We're on in ten minutes," she says. He laughs and releases her but continues to watch her move toward the door.

"Come to the show, Jack, and wait for me afterward." She giggles. He nods and jumps off the bottom step, and I immediately pull back, afraid he'll see me.

It's been over two weeks since I saw Jack at Overtime. Luckily, he missed my panic attack that day. Since then, I've been meeting with Dr. Birch, and my attacks have been less frequent. Maybe she's right about some of the crap she yaps on about. All I care about is that I'm better, so she can carry on with the bullshit as long as I'm not freaking out every day.

I've seen Annie, Stone, and the big tattooed guy they call Fish a couple of times at the restaurant, but not Jack. Maybe he's avoiding me. Naomi says he used to come in all the time. It has to be me. My mind tends to drift to that night when I first met him in the bathroom at Stone's party. If I'm honest with myself, I actually think about him a lot. He's definitely hot. And sexy. Yes, hot and sexy with a gorgeous smile. Those damn lips of his form a perfect lop-sided grin. Hmm… so freaking beautiful.

I turn to move back under the awning but forget about the small step leading to the sidewalk. My foot catches, and damn, it hurts when I hit the ground. Before I can stand, a strong grip around my waist pulls me up.

"You okay?" I would recognize that voice anywhere—Jack.

"Yeah, I'm good. Thanks." He releases my waist, and I take two steps back until my body hits the brick wall.

"Jovie."

"Yeah, that's me," I say, brushing off the knees of my pants. I'm thankful I decided on my skinny jeans and boots tonight and not a skirt.

"You shouldn't be out here alone after dark. This place isn't safe. Especially for a chick."

"I'm not really alone. Layla should be here any minute. So you can go. I don't need a babysitter."

He takes a step back but doesn't leave.

"There... What's *that*?" I ask.

"What's what?"

"Why are staring at me like that?"

Every time we're together, he spends entirely too much time staring into my eyes. It's like he is trying to look into my soul and figure me out. But why?

He takes a couple of steps closer and places one hand on the brick wall behind me. He leans in until I can feel his breath on my face. His eyes never leave mine.

"Are you an angel?"

"Am I a what? Jack, have you been drinking? Don't lie because I can smell it on your breath."

"I had a couple of drinks, but no, not really." He takes his free hand and moves it through my hair gently. And then he nuzzles his nose into my neck and draws in a deep breath. "Your hair's different and you don't smell like her, but those eyes. Those fucking eyes... they *belong* to her."

"No, Jack, these eyes are mine. And you're really freaking me out. You realize you sound more crazy than drunk, right?"

He pushes off the wall and stands in front of me for a beat before walking toward Southern Stain. When he reaches the sidewalk, he looks over his shoulder, his eyes glaring and lips firm. "Seriously, Jovie, go inside the bar." He continues toward the tattoo shop and walks inside without another word.

"Jovie, what are you doing?" I spin around to see Layla approaching in her little black dress and boots. She looks great. No wonder she snagged a guy in a rock band while I'm stuck being alone.

"Nothing, really. Just talking to Jack."

"Who's Jack?"

"This guy I met at Stone's party a couple of months ago."

"Is he hot?"

"Yeah, I guess, but it doesn't matter. It's not like that."

"What's that supposed to mean?"

"Nothing. I met him at a party. Then I saw him out here, and we talked for about two minutes."

"Where did he go?"

"He went back to Southern Stain. That's where he works." I point to the door next to the bar.

"Oh, my God. Don't tell me. He's one of those super-hot tattoo artists. No wonder you went there to have that tattoo done. You know the one you didn't get."

"He's hot. I already told you that. And I got my belly button pierced instead. Remember, I wanted to wait a little while on the tattoo. He didn't even do my piercing. Annie did."

"Geez, why are you being so defensive? I was just curious. Sorry I even mentioned it," she says.

"Look, I'm the one who snapped. So I'm sorry. Just a little stressed with mid-terms and, you know—life."

"It's all good. Now, come on. Let's go inside. I'm so excited for you to hear the band."

We walk into Jake's Bar and the place is packed. We pay our cover charge, and the bouncer puts the lovely orange bands around our wrists so the bartenders will know not to serve us. I look around the room for familiar faces but don't see any. Maybe that's a good thing. Layla leads me to a table in the back of the bar near the makeshift stage. "Sebastian told me to sit at the table near the back of the stage. He said it's reserved for the band so it's supposed to be empty."

I take a seat at the end of the table next to Layla. "How much longer before they're on?"

She looks at the time on her phone. "Any minute now. It's eight o'clock."

The lights dim, and I watch four extremely attractive people step onto the stage. The crowd goes crazy. The lead singer welcomes everybody, and then the music starts. They're good. Really good. But since this is my first time to see a band play live, I don't have much to compare them to. I look at Layla, and she is melting in her seat as she watches her man jump around the stage with his guitar.

Nocturnal Revolution is a local band that has gained popularity by performing at many bars near campus. Layla mentioned to me earlier that the group consists of four cousins. Drake, Sebastian, Ryker, and Ivy. Drake, the lead singer, is the oldest at twenty-seven. He's married with two kids. Ryker and his twin sister, Ivy, are twenty-four. He plays drums and she plays the keyboard. Finally, Layla's new boyfriend and the lead guitar player is Sebastian. He's the baby of the group at twenty-one.

I'm lost in the sound of Drake's smoky voice as my thoughts drift back to Jack. Something is going on with him. I just wish I knew what. Even though he was drunk earlier tonight, he was very adamant that I reminded him of someone. I know when people are drunk they are supposed to be more honest. So, apparently, I do look like either somebody he knows or somebody he used to know. It's weird, but I'm sure it happens all the time. Just not to me.

I feel a hand on my shoulder, and then a slender female body slides into the chair next to mine. Naomi. "Hey, girlie, what's up?" she asks, leaning in closer so I can hear her.

"Not much. Just glad to have my nose out of the books for one night." I motion toward Layla, who is in a Sebastian-induced daze.

Naomi looks at her before she lets out a chuckle. "She's got it bad."

"I have to agree with that."

Half an hour later, the music stops. The crowd cheers after Drake announces they will take a ten-minute break. Suddenly our table is surrounded by girls waiting to get close to the guys in the band. However, they are not too concerned because the three of them take their time getting drinks from the bar before making their way to the table. I focus my attention on Ivy, who is still at the bar. She laughs loudly at something the bartender says, and it's then I realize that it's the same laugh I heard coming from the alley earlier tonight. At that time, all of my attention was focused on Jack and not the female he was talking to—but that laugh. It was Ivy.

"Jovie, have you been introduced to the guys in the band?" Naomi asks.

"No. Do you know them?"

"Yeah. They used to come into the restaurant a lot, but since they've been playing more shows, they haven't been in as much," she says. First, she introduces me to Drake and then Ryker. Her eyes move to Sebastian's empty chair.

"They went to the back," Ryker says. *Of course, they did.*

"I guess Layla can introduce you two later—once she returns from whatever it is she's doing in the back."

I personally don't want to think about or discuss what they are doing in the back. But I'm sure I'll get an ear full when she gets home tonight. There's nothing worse than hearing about somebody's sex life when mine is nonexistent.

Naomi looks toward the bar and makes eye contact with the bartender. She nods twice. Like it's some kind of secret code for her drink order. He grabs a glass and fills it with ice. Then smiles at her before grabbing a bottle of liquor off the top shelf.

"So, who's the bartender?"

"That's Jake. He's getting my drink now. Do you want anything?"

I hold up my wrist sporting my lovely orange band. "Oh, yeah. I forgot. Sorry."

"Naomi, I'm so glad you made it." Ivy. Her voice sounds just like her laugh. Annoying. She's leaning against our table sipping on a beer. She's pretty. I have to give her that, but she doesn't leave much to the imagination with the outfit she's wearing. Her hair's a dark red and is about the length of mine. She's tall. Much taller than I am—about five-foot-nine. She has big round pale green eyes with high cheekbones. She's wearing a form-fitting gray dress with thigh-boots that add about two inches to her height. The dress is off the shoulder—long sleeve and with not much room for those fake boobs.

"Y'all sound great. It's been a while since I've seen the band, but I'm really impressed," Naomi says.

"Thanks, I guess all of the hard work is finally paying off." Ivy looks over at me before she asks, "Who's this... a new groupie?" Before either of us can answer, she continues, "Sorry, chicka. All the guys in our band are taken. Except for my brother, Ryker, and he's not interested. So you can move on. I heard that Reckless Fury's lead singer just got dumped. Maybe you can check him out. They're playing here next Tuesday night. I might even be so kind as to introduce you." She laughs. That fucking laugh. I want to throat punch this fucking bitch. It has nothing to do with the fact that she's most likely fucking Jack. Even if she is, it doesn't matter because I'm sure she's not the only one he's screwing.

"Hmm... just curious. Ivy, right?" She gives me a half eye roll and sighs.

"Why are you such a—"

Naomi cuts me off. "Ivy, this is Jovie. She's here with Layla—Sebastian's date. To answer your question—no, she's not a groupie. So you can stop being such a bitch." Ivy looks down her nose at me and opens her mouth to speak just as Jack shows up at our table.

"Hey, baby, you miss me?" Jack stumbles up from behind and wraps his arms around Ivy's waist. He kisses her neck and she twirls around.

"Of course, I did. We're about to go back on, so wait for me after the show." She pulls on his neck bringing his lips to hers. He smiles through the kiss and releases a loud moan.

Ivy ends the kiss before sauntering back to the stage. I turn toward Naomi to ask her why she cut me off—because I can take up for myself. I'm not helpless. But she's no longer sitting beside me. Jack is. He's turned the chair sideways—facing directly toward me.

What the hell?

I wish he would go away. I can't take any more of *him*—at least not tonight.

"What do you want, Jack?"

"Nothing. Just hanging out. Gonna listen to the band for a bit."

"The band is that way." I point toward the stage. He looks at the band over his shoulder and then back at me.

"I don't have to see them to hear them."

"Fine. Do whatever you want. I'm leaving."

Naomi and Layla are sitting at the bar with a couple of guys I don't know. I'll text Layla once I'm in my car to let her know I'm gone. I don't want her to worry. As I push my chair back to stand, a strong hand wraps around my wrist.

"Please, let go of my arm. I'm leaving."

"No, stay. I'm headed out." I look back at him, and he immediately looks away. Great. Now he's avoiding eye contact. There are things I want to say to him, but I don't. Because being a bitch won't make me feel any better. It will only complicate the awkward relationship we already have. He staggers to the exit door without another look.

CHAPTER 11

JACK

"OPEN UP!" I holler as I kick the screen of the back door of Fish's warehouse. I guess, technically, it's an art gallery, not to mention his home. But it was originally a warehouse.

"Give me a damn minute. Don't be so loud. I just put Gemma down for a nap," he says as he pushes open the door. "You could've made two trips. There's no reason to risk damaging the art by bringing everything in at once."

"Oh, this isn't everything. There's plenty more in the Jeep."

I walk inside, and Fish directs me toward a large oblong table to the right. He helps me free my arms by carefully placing each painting on the table. After two more trips to my Jeep, all my paintings are where they belong—in an art gallery.

He said only ten, but I couldn't help myself. What he doesn't display, I'll pick up before the show. I'm such a fucking rookie, but that will change. Soon.

Fish drags over another table and begins sorting through my paintings, organizing them. He smiles. He nods. Sometimes he raises his eyebrows but never says a word. It's killing me not knowing what he's thinking.

"Hey, this one is good."

"No, not that one." Shit, I didn't mean to bring it.

"That's the chick from Overtime—the waitress that you aren't into. Right?"

"Yeah, Jovie."

"She's beautiful. So, what's the story, and, this time, I want the truth."

"No story, she just reminded me of someone. So, I sketched her from memory and then put on a coat of paint. It's mostly her eyes," I say as Fish pulls the canvas in a little closer to get a better look.

"Piper," he whispers.

"Exactly." I feel better now that somebody else sees it too, and I know it's not all in my head. Sometimes it's hard for me to remember what Piper really looked like. When I can't remember, the guilt consumes me, and I'm taken back to that night. Every. Damn. Time.

And now, this chick has stirred up feelings inside of me I had forgotten even existed. I'm not sure what it is. But I do know it's not something I want to explore. Because judging from my past… that shit never ends well. Just thinking about what happened the other night outside of Jake's makes me cringe. I know I made her uncomfortable… I was drunk, and she was too damn sexy. I lost it for a minute, and that's not something I'm willing to accept. I don't like feeling out of control. And Jovie definitely makes me feel out of control.

"You said to only bring ten, but as you can see, I brought more. I'm kind of indecisive and figured you could choose the ones you thought had the most potential," I say while taking Jovie's portrait from him.

"You have a lot of good pieces. But I think I'm gonna go with the figurative art. These are great. Linen canvas—nice. Single faceless bodies dressed in clothes that portray their personalities."

"Yeah. These are my favorites, too," I say.

"So, what's the theme? Loneliness?"

He looks at me over one of my paintings. I know what he's insinuating. *No, I'm not fucking lonely!*

"Don't go there, man. I appreciate everything you're doing, but I'm not like you. Loneliness is my friend. It gives me room to breathe."

The truth about my art may not be relevant to anybody else, but it means so much to me. It's about loneliness to a certain extent. But mostly, it's about all the men and women I share my art with on a daily basis. Those people come into the shop with a story to tell. A story that is so important to them that they want it told on their skin. Helping my customers search for the right design is one reason my job is so cool. Everyone has a story to tell. Whether they know it or are searching for it doesn't matter. What's important is that they're expressing it through art. This is true with my paintings, too. The faceless figures on the canvas appear to be lonely, but they aren't sad. They are searching for their story—at the beach, in the mountains, on a highway, in the sky, or just sitting in a chair. Their life. Their story. It's important to me.

"Hey, man, if the loneliness thing works for you. Then, that's your business. But what's important now is getting everything lined up for the showing."

"I know. I just want to make a good impression."

"You will. Just remember to wear a suit and bring a date. It's all about the presentation."

"I'll bring Annie." She's not only my best friend but also my go to date.

"No, you won't. She has a date."

"The showing is almost a month away. How does she have a date?"

"She met one of my clients a couple of weeks ago when she was watching Gemma. He asked her, and she said yes. That simple."

"I guess I'll bring Ivy."

"You're still fucking her, aren't you?"

I nod slightly and look away. He doesn't approve of Ivy and my non-relationship fucking. Her twin brother, Ryker is a friend of ours and Fish knows, one day everything with Ivy is going to blow up and cost me my friendship with her brother. But I can't worry about what might be because the here and now is so much more important.

"What am I supposed to do? She can't keep her hands out of my pants."

"You're supposed to say no and walk away."

"Have you seen her? Tell me you could say no and walk away."

"You don't have a problem walking away from Jovie. Didn't we just recently have this conversation?"

"Look. That's different. Ivy doesn't bring back memories of my past. She doesn't take my breath away every time I look in her eyes. Ivy rides my dick and then walks away. Until the next time. No strings, no questions, or even random texts. She's fucking perfect."

We load my remaining paintings into the Jeep without saying another word. I need to apologize to Fish. For my behavior today as well as for the other day at Overtime. I've been a real ass lately. And it all started after the night I met Jovie in Stone's bathroom. Reason enough to stay away from her. I climb in my Jeep and start the engine. Fish taps on my window, so I roll it down. Before he has a chance to say anything, I spill my guts all over his driveway.

"Look, man, I'm sorry I've been acting like such a dick. The other day at Overtime was unacceptable, and today, well, today I just said more than I should. Talking about Piper kinda does this to me. Once I get started, I fall back to that night and let the guilt take over. Then you mention dating and something real, and I get fucking pissed. But it's not you or your fault. So we're good, right?"

"Always, man, plus I usually just ignore your babbling ass anyway." He throws his head back and laughs. Apologizing to Fish is easy. Now apologizing to Jovie is gonna be a little more difficult, but it has to be done.

"Thanks, man. I really appreciate what you're doing. And also, the fact that you're okay with me even though I'm mostly an ass."

"It's cool. Oh, and Jack…"

"Yeah."

"Maybe you meeting Jovie is a good thing. It's possible she is just what you need. Piper is gone, and she's never coming back. And I haven't seen you really let a chick get to you since her. And Jovie, she's getting to you. Even if her eyes resemble Piper's, let it go. It's nothing but your mind playing tricks on your heart."

"I get it, man. It's just hard to let go. To free my heart and give it permission to love. Or even to live a so-called normal life, but… I'll think about it."

"And there's one more thing. I was debating whether to tell you, but I think you need to know. In case…"

"In case…what?" I ask.

"In case you run into him somewhere or… look, Caleb's back in town."

"How do you know?" Fucking unbelievable.

"Dane from over at The Hard Ink told me last week."

"Is that where he's working?"

"Yeah. He's been there about a month."

"Thanks for the warning, but it's all good," I say.

All good, my ass. What the hell is *he* doing back? Seven fucking years and that son-of-a-bitch is back in Houston—after what he did and the lives he destroyed. He has a lot of fucking nerve. I roll up my window, and I back out of my parking space.

Fish shakes his head as he walks back toward the porch. When he turns away, I stop the Jeep in front of the gallery. I slam my fists against the steering wheel until my knuckles ache. Caleb. I can say I actually hate that motherfucker. Why'd Fish even tell me? Can't I have just one day when everything goes right?

I refuse to focus on Caleb. He is a part of my past life. He'll never be anything more. So, I'm going to pretend that Fish didn't just drop a load of shit in my lap on this beautiful sunny fall day. My plan is to apologize to Jovie so I can have some kind of closure with this random chick who I barely know. I'll forget her and then focus on my art, my career, and my future—because those are the things I need in my life. A truck moves in behind me with its horn blaring, telling me to move my Jeep. I let off the brake and move forward, leaving all thoughts of Caleb behind me.

CHAPTER 12

SEVEN YEARS AND SEVEN MONTHS EARLIER

JACK

I GRAB THE antiseptic spray and give the handle a couple of pumps above Caleb's back. The mist settles on the new fire-breathing dragon, and I quickly wipe it clean. Perfection. I fucking love what I do. Even if it's only part time while I'm in school, it gives me the grounding I need to function in everyday life.

"Get the mirror, man. Take a look at your finished piece. It's fucking great." Caleb picks up the mirror from my workstation and turns so his back is facing the full-length mirror. He studies his now finished product. His eyes draw into a squint as he twists and turns so he can see the entire design that takes up over half of his back. It's taken us months to get this piece finished, but looking at it now, it was worth the wait.

"You fuckin killed it, man."

I can't help but feel a sense of pride when a client is happy with my work. Even if this particular client is my co-worker and friend. Caleb and I met here at Southern Stain the beginning of last year. It was our first year of college. We were young, but both had some experience with ink and art. I was lucky enough to shadow some great artists back home in Dallas and Caleb did the same in Little Rock. We did a short apprenticeship after we arrived in Houston, and over the last year, our friendship has grown substantially.

"Thanks, but you designed it. I just reproduced it."

"Yeah, yeah, yeah, my modest friend. Look, I'm gonna head out. I've got some shit to take care of before tonight."

"What's going on tonight?" I ask.

"Not much. Gonna hang out next door at Jake's. Maybe fuck the new waitress. Scarlett, I think is her name. Why don't you meet me there around ten? I'm pretty sure Tara's working. Maybe you guys can rekindle that thing you had going on last summer. "

"Can't do it."

"Why, what's up? You're not working. What could possibly be more important than hanging out with me at your favorite bar? Or should I ask who could possibly be more important?

"I have plans with Piper. I think she wants to see some movie."

"I can't believe you're still dating her. How long has it been? Seven or eight months?"

"No, five months. And why can't you believe we're still together?"

"I don't know. I've just never known you to actually date somebody."

"She's different, man. I mean, I don't know where this is headed, but I'm definitely enjoying the ride."

"I just hate to see you tie yourself down, but if Piper makes you happy, then by all means, keep doing whatever it is you're doing." He laughs.

"You should try it. You know, settling down. It's better than spending every night searching for the next hook-up."

"Maybe for you, but for me—searching is not a problem." He grabs his t-shirt and throws it over his shoulder before heading toward the door.

"If you change your mind, man, you know where to find me. And bring Piper along. I'm sure she'd enjoy hanging out with the guys."

"Maybe next time. See you around," I say as he walks out the door.

"You know Caleb?" Piper asks as she walks into my station just as Caleb is leaving.

"Yeah, why?"

"He's one of your clients?"

"Kinda, but he works here too. How do you know him?" I ask.

"I had a couple of classes with him last semester. But I don't really know him."

"He just invited us to hang out with him and some guys from work tonight, next door at Jakes," I say.

"That sounds like fun." She walks over to the bench and sits next to me.

"Are you sure?"

"Yeah, I'll invite Maddie, if that's okay."

I really don't want to spend my night hanging out with the one person who grates on my nerves more than any other human being does, but if it makes Piper happy, then I guess a few hours with Maddie will be worth it.

"Sure. Invite Maddie."

She pulls her phone out of her bag and walks over to the window. I continue to clean my station. When she's done, she moves toward the door with her phone in hand.

"Maddie's gonna ride with me. We'll meet you there at..."

"Ten," I answer.

"Sounds good. See ya then." She waves and heads out the door.

Tonight will be the first night of many that give me the direct insight of my future. But, unfortunately, I'm too damn blind to see it.

CHAPTER 13

PRESENT DAY

JOVIE

THE RESTAURANT IS empty except for the blond guy in the back corner, but he looks to be finishing up. Lucky for me, it doesn't matter because he belongs to Naomi. Thank God I've got the early shift tonight. I'm exhausted. Too many drunks with wandering hands.

I walk into the break room to get my stuff so I can get the hell out of here. I grab my phone and notice I have three missed calls from my mom. She's dying to talk about Dr. Birch and her clinical evaluation of me. But what dear ole mom doesn't want to hear is the truth. The fact that she and my dad aided in the suppression of my feelings after my sister died. And that's why I'm so fucked up now. She'll hate hearing that anything is her fault. I'm sure she will spend the remainder of the week looking for me a new therapist. One that will tell me what she wants me to hear. At this point, I really don't care what she thinks. I'm better, and mom will just have to deal with the truth. But not tonight. I'm in no mood for her or her shit. She'll have to wait until tomorrow.

As I walk toward the front door, I begin the search for my keys in my never-ending bag. *I really need to get something smaller.* The second I wrap my hands around them, I'm stopped in my tracks by the glass door. My face makes contact first. I'm such a klutz. Great, I'll be sporting a nice purple bruise on my forehead by

61

morning.

"You okay?" Shit. Shit. Shit. Somebody saw me. And not just somebody. A guy. The really cute blond from the back booth.

"Yeah, I'm fine. I was looking for my keys and totally forgot about the door." I glance up at his dark gray eyes.

"Here, let me get the door for you." He pushes it open and stands back so I have plenty of room. Guess he's worried I'll take him down on my way out.

"Thanks."

"Anytime." He smiles and I notice a small dimple in his left cheek. He's cute, but there's no comparison to the tattooed asshole who has taken up residence in my mind. The guy who wishes I were someone else and treats me like…well, nothing… He doesn't actually treat me like anything. One day he notices me, and the next day he doesn't speak. And then he has the nerve to—*why the fuck do I care?* The blond turns and walks toward his car, and I head out in the other direction.

"Jovie." I look to my left and see Jack leaning against his Jeep watching me. What the hell is he doing here? And why does he have to be so damn beautiful? Black t-shirt—just tight enough across his chest to make me want to run my hands over it and take it off. Faded jeans that fit perfectly and dark colored boots that add just enough bad boy to the outfit to make me want him more. If that's even possible. Oh, God, he's perfect. I only wish things weren't so strange between us. But he's here, obviously waiting for me. Maybe this is a good thing. *Maybe.*

"Jack, why are you here?"

"To see you. Is that okay?

"Yes, I guess. What do you want?"

"Come over here. I need to tell you something." He doesn't move an inch. Still leaning against his Jeep, he gives me his lop-sided grin, which makes me want to do terribly bad things to him.

"I'm in a hurry."

"What could you possibly have to do at this time of night

that can't wait ten minutes?"

"Maybe I have a date or am meeting someone to study, or maybe I just have plans. Is that impossible to believe?" Why do I feel the need to assume that he thinks I'm some kind of loser with no life? Because unfortunately, I am.

Instead of airing all my insecurities, I need to channel my confidence, walk over to him, and hear what he has to say. Then turn around and walk away. And hopefully, I will never have to lay eyes on all of his arrogant beauty again. Yeah, that's exactly what I need to do, but what I want to do is throw him down and rip all of his clothes off. Yes. Right here in this parking lot.

He continues to stare holding his signature grin in place. He winks and says, "Of course, anything's possible. I don't doubt that you have something important to do, Jovie. I only want to take a few minutes of your time. And then you can go do whatever it is you have planned."

I don't have any real plans, and I assume he knows it. Unless I count spending two hours with my World Civilization book.

Why do I even care? In reality, I barely know him. We've only had a couple of conversations. He did see me at my worst the first night I met him, but he has been kind enough not to mention it.

Really, what am I worried about? I'm ridiculous. Making more out of a situation than is necessary.

I take a deep breath and tread a little closer. He pushes off the Jeep, and I stop in front of him. Not too close, but close enough that I can smell him. And he smells amazing. Like a fresh shower and aftershave… clean.

There is just enough light for me to see his deep brown eyes. I smile and take another step closer before I say, "You haven't been drinking, have you?"

He turns away for a brief moment before his eyes return to mine. Heat rushes to my cheeks as he moves in closer. He chuckles and says, "No. Not tonight. But that's part of the reason

I'm here."

"You want to drink? We've already closed the bar."

"I'm not here to drink, Jovie. I'm here to apologize for being drunk and making an ass of myself the other night at Jakes."

"Oh." He's apologizing. I guess that's a good thing. I take a step away from him, but my eyes never leave his. I push a strand of curls behind my ear and take in a deep breath.

"You don't have to apologize, Jack. I deal with drunk guys all the time." Shit—that came out wrong. "I mean at work. I'm used to being around a lot of intoxicated people that say and do things they don't mean. So, no worries. It's fine. Actually, it's already forgotten."

"Wow. I'm unforgettable." He closes the gap between us until there's no room to move without feeling his body against mine. The bare skin of my stomach is making this nearness a little more uncomfortable than I would like. Damn these uniforms.

"No, I didn't mean it like it sounded. I just—"

"You just what?" he mumbles.

"Apology accepted. I have plans, remember? Can I leave now?"

"You can leave whenever you want. I'm not keeping you here."

Well, then move away from me and take your incredible smell with you. He's saying one thing, but his actions are showing something completely different. I feel his body touching mine with each breath I take. He's that damn close. Too close.

"See you around, Jack." I turn toward my car, but before I move away, he grabs my wrist spinning me around until I'm facing him.

"I know I said you could leave, but before you do, there's one more thing…"

He places his lips on my cheek. One soft kiss, and then another one, and then he is moving his soft kisses down my neck until he stops at my shoulder.

A shiver races up my spine and need takes over every emotion I own. The ability to control my body is slowly fading. Jack shifts his firm chest forward and releases my wrist. He wraps his arms around my waist lifting me off the ground. I grab his shoulders to keep from falling. And six steps later, I'm sitting on the hood of my car with my legs wrapped around his waist and my hands pressing against his chest. I seem to have lost all thoughts of why I shouldn't be participating in this little charade with him. At this point, I don't care if he's doing this because I remind him of someone else.

Tonight, I'm not going to worry about him or his reasons. I'm only here for me. Besides, Dr. Birch said I needed to get out and meet people. Make new friends. So here I am, on the hood of my car in an empty parking lot making a new friend.

He tilts his head near my ear and whispers, "One more thing…" His breath is heavy as he pauses a beat before continuing. "A kiss, just one kiss before I go."

It's not a question, but a statement. So I don't answer. I can't. I'm lost in this moment of warm skin underneath my touch, the sound of his soft breath on my ear, and the need to take care of the growing ache between my legs.

His lips move slow and steady on my skin until his mouth is on mine. The kiss is soft and light. The clarity of what's happening is lost somewhere within my thoughts. I close my eyes and wrap my legs tighter around his waist, pulling him in until our bodies are connected.

The warmth of his breath and the soft licks of his tongue only intensify the growing tension between us. A soft moan escapes my lips as he pulls his mouth from mine. My eyes open and he's watching—staring into my eyes. The power this one look has is terrifying. And what he sees I'll probably never know. At least not tonight because he releases his hold on me before looking away.

I free my legs from around his waist and scoot myself toward the center of my car to regain my balance. He moves away from me, never losing eye contact. His lips move as if he's trying to mumble something, but there's no sound.

"What, Jack?" Completely ignoring my question, he turns and walks to his vehicle.

"You're leaving?"

"Looks that way." Three fucking words, and then he climbs into his Jeep and drives away.

CHAPTER 14

JOVIE

RYKER. MY DATE for tonight's big event. An art show downtown that's supposed to be some kind of tradition. At least, that's what Layla says. The date—her idea, too. She told me I need to do things other than going to school and work. I want to tell her I do get out and do other things. I meet with Dr. Birch every week to discuss why I'm a fucking wreck, but I don't because she would harass me for details after every appointment. And rehashing my counseling sessions is not something I want to do.

"Ryker is so groovy. You're gonna love him. I just know it." Who the hell says groovy? Oh yeah. My best friend does. She's changing. Since she started dating Sebastian—the guy who plays in the band—she has been talking like she's some kind of hippie. And Sebastian, he clearly doesn't look like any hippie I've ever seen. He has short brown hair with longer bangs that swoop in the front and his face. Let's just say he looks like an all-American pretty boy, not some hippie guitar playing freak in the band they call Nocturnal Revolution.

"I'm sure he's great. I'm just kind of nervous. You know this is my first real date."

She walks out of the bathroom and into her bedroom where I'm perched on the edge of her bed. She has these huge rollers spread all over her head. What the hell? Who even rolls their hair anymore? Change is not always for the best. But who am I to judge? I have enough of my own issues to worry about hers.

67

"What about Liam? Y'all kinda dated."

"No, we didn't. We had sex. And that's after I snuck out of my house at night. There was no dating involved in that relationship."

She walks over to the bed where I'm sitting and plops down beside me. Her eyebrows pull in as she scrunches her nose before saying, "At least you're not a virgin… Thank God you got that task out of the way. Or this date would be nerve-racking."

Who is this person sitting next to me? That statement was borderline bitch. My best friend would never say mean things to me.

"Wow, Layla that was rude. Do you think I'm happy about the fact that I'm nineteen and never been on a date?" At least, I'm not nineteen and having screwed my way through half our high school football team. No, I didn't say it, but I could be a bitch, too. It's easy to be mean and hurtful, but I choose not to. She's lucky I love her.

"No, of course, you're not happy about it. I don't blame you. That's why I'm helping you out. You're my best friend, and I want you to find somebody who makes you as happy as Sebastian makes me."

Can I vomit now, please? Not only does he make her mean, but he has her completely under his spell.

"Thank you, my best friend, Layla. But please don't be a bitch to me."

"I really wasn't trying to be mean. I'm sorry if I hurt your feelings. Now let's find something to wear and get you ready for your big night." She jumps up and hurries to her closet.

* * * * *

I hate to admit it, but Layla was right about tonight. I need this. To let go of my life for one night. No thoughts of school, work, anxiety, or even Dr. Birch. This is so freaking great. We walk out of gallery number five and climb the steep sidewalk toward the last stop on the list. Ryker gently slides his fingers between mine. Handholding. Something I've not done much of until tonight. Liam used to like to lie in bed and hold my hand after sex. But tonight's experience is different. It gives me a sense of warmth and security, even if it's with a guy I only met hours ago.

As we approach the last gallery, I wonder if this will be it for my date and me. Will he ask me out for a second or will he tell me he'll call—and then I never hear from him again? It doesn't matter. I like him, but if he doesn't want to see me again, I'm good with that.

"So are you up for this last gallery?" Ryker asks as we walk up the stairs to the front door.

"Yes, this has been great. I never thought of myself as someone who likes art, but you've opened my eyes to a whole new world."

"To be honest, I'm not much into art. So I don't deserve all the credit for tonight. My cousin, Drake, had these tickets and didn't feel like finding a sitter for his kids, so he gave them to me. But…" he points to the door and finishes, "I'm looking forward to this gallery. It belongs to a buddy of mine, and the paintings on display tonight were done by my sister's boyfriend." He reaches for the handle, pulling it open for me. I release his hand and walk through the door as my mind processes the words that just came out of his mouth.

"Your sister's boyfriend?" The last time I saw Ivy—the bitch—she was hanging all over Jack. And Jack is far from boyfriend material. But now that I think about it, Ivy doesn't look much like girlfriend material, either.

"Yeah, I'll introduce you to him. Do you know my sister Ivy?" His hand finds the small of my back as he guides me through the crowd of art lovers. We weave in and out of people while I search the room for the last person I want to see tonight... Jack.

He's talking to a group of people while pointing to one of the paintings on display. Ivy's glued to his side clinging to every word he says. She laughs and moves a little closer to him. Shit. One more step and she's going to be standing on top of him. He nods to the small crowd as he wraps his arm around Ivy's waist leading her away from the group. She brings her lips to the glass of wine she's holding and tilts it up taking a quick sip. Her eyes are smiling as if she's the happiest fucking person in the world—until she finds me across the room. Bringing the glass down, she looks to my right. Her eyes double in size, and I swear I see fire shoot from her ears. She's pissed. Not because I'm in the same room as she is, but because her brother is standing as close to me as she is to Jack. This situation shouldn't bring any joy to my heart, but it does. Am I ashamed? No. *Not. At. All.* Because if I remember correctly, a few weeks ago, she called me a groupie and said her brother wasn't interested in me. And for the first time in my life, I witness disgust in someone's eyes. And it's directed toward me. She really doesn't like me.

"No, I don't know her. Remember, I'm new around here. If you don't eat at Overtime or sit by me in class, then I don't know you."

"I just thought maybe you had met her at Overtime with Jack. I know the guys from the shop eat there a lot. Or at least, they used to," he says.

"Oh," is the only response I'm giving him. He doesn't need to know that Jack avoids me. Especially after I let him make a fool out of me in the parking lot on the hood of my car. I still can't believe I was so stupid.

"There they are." Ryker motions toward Jack and Ivy before saying, "They're alone, so now's the perfect time for me to introduce you to them."

Ryker leads me across the room with his hand still planted firmly on my lower back. Jack doesn't notice me until we are just inches away. When he finally sees me, he immediately drops his arm from around Ivy's waist. Jack looks away focusing his attention toward the wall of paintings. He's ignoring me. Is it because I remind him of somebody else. Or does he treat all females like this? I remember the day from Southern Stain and the blonde who was crying as she fumbled for her keys. Trying to get away from there or was it Jack she was running from? After all, Jack did have the handprint across his cheek. So perhaps he is a jerk to all females. Except Ivy. And I'm sure that will eventually happen, too.

"Ryker," Ivy says as her eyes scan my body from head to toe. She looks great, but I wouldn't have expected her to look anything short of stunning. Her long red hair is in some kind of updo that probably cost her more than my weekly paycheck. The white dress she's wearing hangs a little shorter than mid-thigh and those silver heels add an extra few inches to her already long legs. But her outer beauty means absolutely nothing to me. It's what she has on the inside that counts. And from what I've seen, it's far from pretty. But who am I to judge. She's my date's sister, so I vow to be on my best behavior. Unless she backs me against the wall, and then I don't care whose sister she is.

"Hey, sis. Looks like the party is still in full swing. I thought by saving Jack's stop for last, the older crowd would have headed home for the night and we could hang out with you guys."

Hang out with them. Umm… no thanks. I'm hoping for a quick hi and then we can continue on our way. Although I would like to see Jack's paintings. After making the rounds at the last five galleries, I'm kind of feeling like an art expert. Well, maybe not an expert, but I've learned something new about myself. Maybe I like to look at paintings. The magical canvases that portray someone's inner vision.

"I didn't realize you were coming tonight. Did you forget to mention it earlier?" Ivy asks.

"No, I didn't forget. You knew that Drake gave me the

tickets." The back and forth bantering between the twins is becoming quite boring. Twins… I look closely at Ivy and then at Ryker, and realize they may be brother and sister, but look nothing alike. Ivy with her red hair, pale skin, and green eyes would be the last person in this room I would choose as Ryker's twin. Although Ivy is very striking, she has nothing on her sandy blond-haired, blue-eyed sibling.

I nudge Ryker with my elbow so he's aware I'm still standing next to him. I don't want to look at Ivy, but I do glance over at Jack. He continues to stare at the wall of paintings as if we're not here.

Ryker finally looks over at me, and then whispers, "Sorry."

I smile so he knows I'm not mad. I really want to leave. Screw looking at the art. I'll be fine not knowing that Jack is probably an amazing artist.

"Ivy—Jack, this is my date, Jovie," he announces. Damn, he thought I meant for introductions. That's the last thing I want. Being introduced to people who didn't want to meet me a first time, much less a second time is not cool. A twitch suddenly takes over my right eye and my face goes numb. Holy fucking shit. Not. Now. My chest grows heavy. My breathing quickens. It's happening. And I can't stop it. The anxiety is taking over my body. The fight or flight mode is kicking in. So I need to run— get away. Leave.

"Jovie, hmm… so I was right. You are a groupie." She looks at Ryker and shrugs. At this point, I couldn't care less about what she thinks of me. I'm also not concerned about anything she has to say, so I search the room for the nearest exit. Whether a bedroom, bathroom or the front door. Just get me the hell out of here. Because if I don't get out of this room, I'm gonna stop breathing. I move out of Ryker's hold and turn away from the group. My legs are shaky, but I manage to walk away. Away from Ryker. Away from Ivy. And away from Jack.

"Jovie, where are you going?" Ryker shouts.

"I'll be back in a minute." My voice is trembling. Please don't follow me. If he does, then I'll have to tell him how screwed up I am. Because if I don't explain it, then he'll believe what he wants.

I turn and rush toward the front door. Outside is where I need to be. Free from walls and people. No banging on a door to let them in. Only open space and me. Room to move—to run if I need to—and most importantly, room to breathe. I reach the door and grab the doorknob. A sense of freedom is so near I can taste it. I turn it to the right and then to the left. The fucking thing won't open. I pull—push—yank and wiggle the handle for what seems like an eternity. Then a hand covers mine. No. No. No. I have to leave. Please let go.

"Let go of my hand." I move my eyes from the hand to the face. Jack.

"Are you okay?" Completely ignoring his ridiculous question, I turn the knob again. This time, the door moves. It opens and to my surprise, he doesn't try to stop me. He releases my hand as I push the door open.

With rapid breathing, I look over my shoulder at his face and say, "Leave me alone. Please, just go back to your date."

As soon as I escape the confinement of the gallery, my body collapses against the railing on the porch. Thankfully, there's no one else around. Only me—surrounded by air and darkness. Finally, I inhale and can breathe again.

CHAPTER 15

JACK

THE DOOR CLOSED and she was gone. Outside alone, having another one of those episodes. It happened so fast. First, the blotchy redness appeared on her neck and face. Then the look of pure terror was apparent in her eyes. She had to get out of this crowd. Away from everyone, including me.

I want to help her. I don't think letting her go outside into the darkness alone is the right thing to do. But that's what she wanted. She asked for me to step back and let her go, so I did. But part of the reason she wanted away from me was probably because of the way I treated her the last time we were together. I left her alone in an empty parking lot. I went there that night to apologize but only made things worse. Such a dick. She probably never wants to see my face again.

"What the hell just happened?"

Ivy. She's pissed. I turn around to face her and instantly regret it. Firm lips and fire in her eyes are not something I've ever seen with her. Jealousy. It doesn't look good on her. We have such a good thing. I hope tonight isn't the night she decides to show her ass and ruin it for the both of us.

"Calm down, Ivy. It's nothing. Just checking on a friend."

"A friend. A fucking friend. Since when did you become friends with the groupie?"

"Groupie?" I ask her in complete confusion.

"Yes, a groupie. A person who follows a band around like a

lost puppy. Hoping to fuck not one but all of the male members."

"I know what a groupie is, Ivy. Why are you calling her one?"

"Because that's what she is. She was at our table a few weeks ago when we played at Jake's, and now she's here with my brother. Following him around like the little slut she is."

"Stop it, Ivy. I mean it. You don't know her—"

"Oh, but you do? Just how well do *you* know her, Jack? Maybe she lusts after tattoo artists, too. Am I right? You fuck her already? Leaving what's left for my brother?" Her voice is harsh—mean—hateful. I've never seen her act this way.

"What the hell is wrong with you?"

"What's wrong with me? Some random girl shows up with my brother, starts to freak out, and you—my date—run after her when she takes off. So you tell me… what's wrong with you?"

Ryker walks by us without making eye contact. He's heading for the door. To find her and make everything better. Make the fear go away. And that pisses me off. Because I want to be the one to make it go away. Not him. Ivy's eyes follow him until he's made it through the door. And then she slings her head back in my direction. Something tells me we aren't done here—or at least, she isn't. But I've had all the shit I'm going to take from her for one night. I grab her arm and pull her out of the crowded room into Gemma's play area. I release her arm as I shut the door. She presses her back against the wall and glares into my eyes.

"That's enough, Ivy. I don't owe you anything. I'm not your boyfriend. It shouldn't matter to you what I do. We have sex. Great sex. So don't start with the jealousy bullshit and ruin a good thing."

Pushing herself off the wall, she walks over to the window and leans against the sill. Facing away from me, she raises her voice slightly as she asks, "Is that what you think this is about? You think I'm jealous of that girl?" She throws her head back and laughs. "I'm not jealous of her or any other female, for that matter."

"If it's not jealousy, then what the hell is it? I've never seen you act like this before. Like a crazed beast out for blood."

She turns and faces me before saying, "Embarrassed. You embarrassed me tonight in front of my brother for starters. And then in front of friends. Fish and Stone were standing in the back corner watching, along with Annie and her date. Not to mention all the people mingling around pretending to look at your paintings. When they were really watching you as you practically sprinted away from me to chase down someone else's date."

"Look, Ivy. I didn't mean to embarrass you. It's just that..." I can't tell her I've seen Jovie like this before or that I have an overwhelming need to help her when she freaks out.

"It's just what, Jack?" She walks over to me and rests her hands on my shoulders. She presses her lips to mine for a quick kiss. Then she leans in placing her cheek next to mine and whispers, "Don't for one second think that you're the only guy I'm fucking. And never again accuse me of an emotion that I could never possess. Jealousy is for the weak." Pulling away from me, she moves toward the door. "This night is over. At least, it is for me. I hope you sold some paintings." She stops before reaching the door and smirks in my direction. "And sex. Yeah, we won't be having any of that tonight. So if that is the only reason you brought me... then sorry?" She shrugs her shoulders and laughs before strolling out the door.

I've never been so happy to watch someone walk out of a room in my entire life. She tried to fucking ruin my night, but at least, Fish introduced me to the groups of potential buyers early and often, so I was able to circulate through the crowd for a couple of hours before Ryker and Jovie showed up. I'm not blaming them for Ivy's shit show, but Fish's warning was spot on. 'Things ending badly' is an understatement on how things are going to end between Ivy and me. I hope she gets the message and tonight's the end. But I have a bad feeling she's not done with me yet. She's not only pissed at me but has it out for Jovie. Bitch is an understatement of how ruthless she can be if she puts her mind to it.

I head out of the playroom and into the thinning crowd of people.

"What just went down between you, the twins, and that hot waitress from Overtime?" Fish asks as he approaches me in the hallway.

"Just a misunderstanding."

"Sure looked like more than a misunderstanding from where I was standing."

"Okay. You were right. Is that better?"

"Right about what?" he asks.

"This thing with Ivy is a bad idea. I saw a side of her tonight I didn't like. She says I embarrassed her, but it looked like jealousy to me. But none of that matters now. She's gone."

"Right, huh? I like the sound of that." Fish laughs and looks toward the door. I shift over a little and turn my head to get a good view of what he's looking at—or who he's looking at. Hopefully, Ivy's not back. Thankfully, she's not. It's Ryker.

Looking directly at me, he asks, "Hey, guys, either of you seen my sister?"

"Not in the last ten minutes. Why? Everything okay?"

"Yeah. I'm about to take Jovie home. I needed to talk to her for a sec before we head out."

Glancing over at Fish, I let my eyes travel from him to the hallway. He doesn't say a word but watches me intently. I'm so damn predictable.

"I think she's in the restroom. Maybe check there. Down the hall, around the corner, the last door on the left," I say.

"Thanks, man." Ryker heads toward the hallway.

"You're a liar. A terrible fucking liar. She left, didn't she?" Fish asks.

"Yeah, but I only bought myself a couple of minutes. I'll be right back. And when I return, I'll be ready to hear about how all my paintings sold at my first showing."

"Just go and hurry your ass up so you don't get caught," he says.

I almost trip over my feet as I rush toward the door. Managing to keep my balance, I make it outside onto the porch. Staggering down the steps, I search for a petite dark haired beauty in a black dress. I see movement out of the corner of my eye, but I realize it's not her when I hear a male voice followed by female laughter. Maybe she's in Ryker's truck waiting, but it's not parked here. There's not much room for parking and every space is full. No truck in sight. He probably parked down the street. As I turn to walk down the hill toward the other galleries, the sound of a female clearing her throat stops me in my tracks. It's her. She's leaning against a tree on the edge of the property.

"Jovie?" I ask before approaching her.

"It's me," she says.

I walk over toward the tree, giving her enough space so I don't make her feel uncomfortable. But she's still close, so close I feel her breath on my face. She's quiet and composed. Her breathing is steady. It makes me wonder whether or not she took something to bring her back down to this level of calmness. I need to talk—tell her what's weighing on my mind. But I don't have a lot of time. Ryker will be out any minute and take her away... with him.

"Hey, you okay?" I ask.

"Of course, I'm okay, Jack. Why wouldn't I be?"

"When you took off earlier, I was afraid you were having another one of those... you know, like you did the first night I met you." Damn, I'm an idiot. I still don't know what to say to her. My tongue trips over words as if I've never spoken to anyone before. She needs to know that I only want to help.

"It's called an anxiety attack. And yes, I did have one earlier,

78

but the good news is they usually only last about ten minutes. A lot of time not nearly that long. Then I'm fine until the next one."

"Anxiety?"

"Yes, it is caused by—well, things out of my control. Look, Jack, I would rather not discuss this with you right now. I just want to go home."

"Jack?" I step away from Jovie turning to face the sound of the male voice. I know who it is before my eyes meet his.

"I'm leaving. Just stopping by to check on Jovie. You know, since she's out here alone. Just wanted to be sure she's okay."

"She's fine," Ryker says. Then he redirects his attention to Jovie before I have the chance to speak.

"I'm sorry about tonight. Really wanted you to have fun because I know you're busy and don't get out much," he says to Jovie.

"I did have a good time. It's the most fun I've had… well… since I can remember. Please don't blame yourself, Ryker," she says.

Yeah, I'm the third wheel. Imposing on their privacy or whatever, but I'm not walking away until they leave, or they ask me to go. Yes, I know this is a dick move… again.

Ryker clasps Jovie's hand with his. She pushes off the tree and they walk several feet away, leaving me standing alone. Like an idiot. I guess this is my cue to leave. I really want to go back in to discuss the night with Fish, but I'm not ready to walk away from her. They inch further away so I decide just to let it go tonight and head home.

I pull my keys out of my pocket and proceed down the incline toward my Jeep. Once I arrive at my ride, I turn back a little to get one last look at the couple before I head out. Jovie wraps her hands around his neck and leans in for a hug. When she pulls back, he kisses her slowly on the cheek before backing away. Her hands release his neck and slide down his arms until their hands lock together. I shake my head with agitation, disgust, or jealousy. Hell, I don't even know at this point. I just need to go—because I don't want to watch them leave together. I climb into the Jeep, start the ignition, and roll down the window.

I find comfort in the fact that I know tonight's date was more than likely a fix-up. Her roommate is dating Ryker's cousin. Besides, she didn't really seem that into him. What the fuck am I doing? Why do I care?

A hand slams on the panel of my open window startling me out my current thoughts and bringing me back to the here and now.

"Ivy's gone. She wasn't in the restroom or anywhere else in the house. I don't know why she left or how she got home, but you need to fix whatever broke between you two tonight," Ryker says.

"There's nothing to fix. It's all good," I say. She needs to tell him about our situation. I'm not going there with her brother.

"She called me before I got back outside. Dad's in the ER again. He had another flare up with his lungs. So mom called an ambulance. Anyway, she's at the hospital now with my parents. I'm heading that way," he says.

"What about Jovie? Where is she?"

"Naomi and Stone are still inside. They offered to give her a ride home. I would take her myself, but the hospital is only four blocks over. She didn't want me to have to go out of my way. You know, she's fucking great. If things go as well on our second date, then maybe we can double with you and Ivy."

I nod in agreement before saying, "Yeah, maybe." *No. Never happening.*

Other than that last statement, my night just got a whole lot better. Jovie's still here and her date is leaving. I try to hold back a smile, but it's difficult.

"Hope your dad's all right, man. Tell Ivy I'll catch up with her tomorrow."

"Will do," he says as he walks down the hill toward the

parking lot.

I wait. And wait. Until Ryker is no longer in sight. After rolling up my window, I open the door and jump out. This is wrong. So wrong.

I walk back toward the gallery. No Jovie standing near the tree. I bet she's back inside. As I make my way up the steps, I spot her. Leaning against the wall near the entrance.

"Hey, I thought you'd be inside with Naomi." She's beautiful. If I could only get my shit together. Maybe I could help her with whatever is causing her to have all of this anxiety. Honestly, it would take a lot more than just getting my shit together to fix someone else.

"Nope, I find it more calming out here. Alone." She looks away.

"I take that as a hint for me to leave. Am I right?" I ask.

"Do whatever you want, Jack. Leave—stay—it's totally up to you."

"Why don't you let me take you home so you're not stuck waiting. There are still a lot of people here, and Naomi and Stone may be a while."

"After the few times we've been together, do you honestly believe I want to be alone with you again?"

"Look, you're right. I'm a total jerk. Not to mention that I suck at apologizing. Just give me one more chance. I promise I'll take you home and that's it. No staring into your eyes, no accusing you of being someone else, and absolutely no kissing."

"No kissing?" Her face flushes a light shade of red.

"Nope. No kissing." I smile and wink.

She slowly walks toward me. And when she stops, her lips are near mine.

"No kissing, Jack. Are you sure about that." She pulls her bottom lip between her teeth before looking down.

What the fuck is she doing to me? My dick decides to push against my pants. Out. He wants out, but that's not happening tonight. Or anytime soon with her.

"Yes. I'm positive. So, you ready to go?" I ask.

She lifts her head, looking into my brown eyes with her glassy blue ones. Shit. Did I hurt her feelings again? Surely, she's not gonna cry. I don't do crying. She takes a deep breath and smiles.

"Okay, let's get out of here," she says before she turns and walks toward my Jeep.

She makes her way around to the passenger side and pulls the door open.

"Wait, there's something I forgot to ask when I offered you a ride home."

"What's that?"

"Can you drive?"

"Of course, I can. You know that. You've seen my car. Actually, you're quite familiar with the hood." Those glassy eyes are glaring now. Directly at me.

"I didn't mean *can* you. I guess I meant will you?"

"Will I drive?"

"That's the question," I mumble loud enough for her to hear.

"Why? It's your Jeep and plus, I've never driven anything this big, but you know that. You've seen my car."

"Just keep throwing daggers, Jovie. I was wrong for leaving you on the hood of the car that night. I'm sorry. I can't say it enough. Because there aren't enough ways to say 'I'm sorry' to make up for what I did." I hang my head.

She leaves the passengers door open and walks around to where I'm standing. She holds her hand out in front of me with her palm facing up.

"What?" I ask.

"Give me the keys. I'll drive."

I reach into my pocket, grab my keys, and gently place them in her hand.

"This is kinda crazy, but if you insist on me driving, then that's your business," she says as she walks around to the driver's side. We both climb in, latch our seatbelts, and are on our way.

We ride in silence the whole way to her apartment. I didn't try to start a conversation, but I wasn't the only one. She didn't speak or even look my direction one time.

I can't let tonight end like this, but before I can think of the right thing to say, she asks, "So why did you want me to drive? I've been racking my brain this entire time and can't figure it out. I know you drive, so why not tonight. You're not drunk. I don't smell alcohol, so I don't think you had anything to drink. I just think it's kind of weird."

"It's a long story. One that I would rather not talk about tonight. You know how you don't want to talk about your anxiety episodes with me?"

"I get it. It's fine. I'll see you around." She opens the door and hops out before walking toward apartment 126A. She stops just a few feet away from her door and turns to face me. God, what is it about this chick? She takes my fucking breath away.

"Thanks for getting me home safely," she says.

"You're welcome. And Jovie…"

"Yeah?"

"I truly am sorry about… everything."

She smiles before turning toward her door and walking inside.

CHAPTER 16

JOVIE

EMERALD FOREST CEMETERY. The final resting place of my sister. I hate it when people say shit like that. Final resting place. The only thing resting here is what's left of her decaying body. I'm really hoping I can do this. Dr. Birch wanted me to come here—to visit my deceased sibling. Those are her words, not mine. She says it will help with the closure bullshit. And if this doesn't work, then she will refer me to a psychiatrist for medication therapy. Yay for me! Medicated is the one thing I don't want, but if it stops the suffering, then I'm about ready to say bring on the drugs. All I'm asking for is normalcy. An ordinary life. Too much to ask for? I'm tired of living every day in fear. Because to be honest, the fear of when the anxiety will strike again is causing me a multitude of problems. I barely eat. Sleep is a luxury. School is school and my grades are suffering. I spend most of my time alone because I don't want anyone else to witness my crazy.

"Do you want me to go with you to the gravesite?" Layla asks.

Dr. Birch recommended I not come here alone. So, I did what I should've done in the beginning. I told Layla. Everything. I told her the truth about the attacks before leaving Brownsboro and about the recent ones. As if that wasn't enough, I let my mouth overflow about Jack, the hood of my car, him making me drive myself home while he rode beside me, and about Ivy— queen of the bitches. I even threw in the part about her running a close second to Ivy in the bitch department. My little truth session made me feel a bit guilty, but it worked. She understood and apologized. I seem to be getting a lot of apologies lately.

"Yes, please. If you'll just walk with me and wait back a little ways so I can have privacy, but also, know you're still near."

"Anything you want. I'm here for you. You're my best friend, Jovie. I love you."

She smiles as we both get out of my car. I pull the folded paper out of my pocket. The directions to her grave. I've only been here once. The day she was buried. After that, my parents never let me come back. They come every year on her birthday. But never talk about it. I often wonder if they talk about her to each other.

Last week, I called my mom to ask her where the cemetery was located. She raised seven kinds of hell. She said me visiting the gravesite was a mistake. It would only make my anxiety worse and blah, blah, blah. So I hung up on her. Then I called my dad. He went through the same bullshit speech as she had, but he gave me the name and the number of the man who takes care of her grave. Told me to call him for directions. So that's what I did. Mr. Robert Estes, the gravesite keeper of my one and only deceased sibling, told me everything I needed to know.

"I know you do. And I love you, too. Thank you." She falls behind me letting me get several steps ahead of her. I glance over my shoulder and say, "I don't even remember the date she died. I mean, I remember the day and everything, but I don't know the date. I was so young and my parents, well, they never brought it up. The only date ever discussed was her birthday. Because they fly out here every year on that day."

"Don't you feel guilty—not even for a second. You were only a kid. Your life fell apart, and you had no one to pick up the pieces. Besides, you'll know the date once we get there. It'll be on the tombstone."

"Oh yeah. I completely forgot. See? I am so glad you're here with me. Things are better already."

I look down at the directions and continue my hike up slope after slope until I arrive at my destination. As I wrap my arms around my waist, I drop to my knees. October 25, 2008. The day I lost my sister and my best friend. Sissy. Just as it says on the tombstone. Mom and Dad put it there for me. Yet never allowed me to see it. So now I'm here, putting the pieces of my life back together bit by bit. I place my hand on the tombstone and lower my head.

"Why did you leave me?" Tears stream down my face as I take in a ragged breath.

"I've needed you so many times. Like now. I'm falling apart. Alone," I bellow.

"You said you loved me. I was a little girl and hung onto every promise you made. And then you were gone. Taking every promise with you. You left one night and never came home."

I tilt my head back and take in a deep breath. I gasp and then scream. I'm straining to pull air into my lungs. They're not working. My lungs—I can't get any air. My chest is heavy. Something is happening to me. And it doesn't feel like anxiety. It feels like death. I'm dying.

"Breathe, just breathe," I chant.

"One, two, three, four, five." It's not working. I'm not getting better. I need help—please.

"Layla… Layla," I scream before everything goes black.

* * * * *

I'm breathing. Inhale then exhale. I place my hand on my chest. It rises and falls. I'm alive. Where am I? I'm lying on something rough. Sandpaper? I pry my eyes open—darkness is surrounding me. I'm greeted with nothing but an annoying beeping noise.

"Layla, are you here? Layla," I mumble.

Movement from the back corner of the room gives me

reassurance that someone is here.

"I'm here. Do you want the light on?" she asks.

"Yes, please. Where am I?"

"The hospital. Are you feeling okay?" Layla asks as she turns the overhead light on.

Brightness fills the dull room. Gray walls and a curtain separates me from the hallway.

"Yes, I'm fine. Why am I here?" I look at Layla. She looks exhausted. No makeup, sweatpants, t-shirt, and her hair on top of her head in a messy bun.

"You fainted at the cemetery. I called the ambulance because I was so scared. I couldn't get you to wake up. I thought you were dead," she utters.

Her eyes are red and swollen. I can tell she's been crying. Because of me. I feel terrible for this whole ordeal.

"Am I in a room? Why is there a curtain for the door?"

"You're in the ER. The nurse told me to get her when you wake up so the doctor can come in. I think he's gonna let you go home."

"Why did I pass out? What's wrong with me?"

"The doctor said you were dehydrated. That's why you have an IV in your hand. For the fluids. He said dehydration combined with the anxiety probably caused you to faint. They gave you something to sleep and ran some tests. Everything is okay. He also said you should take better care of yourself. But that's no secret, right?"

I nod and stretch my arms above my head.

"Will you get the nurse so we can leave?" I ask.

"Sure. I'm ready to get out of this place, too. Oh, just so you know, I called your parents. I was scared not to call them. They want you to call them so they can decide whether they need to fly out. I told them no, but your mom freaked out. So, if you don't give her a call, she'll probably be here in the morning."

"Great, just what I need. More freaking stress. You know

how she is," I say.

Layla walks into the hallway and returns shortly with a tall, slender middle-aged woman—the nurse who is in charge of my care. The doctor comes in shortly after. They both go over the same stuff Layla had already told me. He gives me a prescription for Xanax, tells me to follow up with my psychologist, and possibly a psychiatrist.

Once I'm home, I fall into my bed and cry. I cry for my sister, for my mom and dad, and for myself. The tears fall and fall and fall. Until there's no more. I want to be free from the fear that chases me daily.

Layla and I decide to tuck this day away and not speak of it ever again.

Tomorrow will be better.

It has to be.

CHAPTER 17

JOVIE

"SABRINA JUST SAT someone in the back booth—of your section." I glance to the right as Naomi walks by. Sabrina is the hostess and obviously, an idiot. My shift is almost over. What's wrong with her?

"I leave in ten. Do you wanna take it or see if Nikki wants it?" Nikki is the bartender tonight, but she will wait the occasional table. I stand on my tiptoes looking over the row of tables toward the back of the restaurant. It's so damn dark back there that it's impossible to tell how many bodies are occupying the booth.

"Neither, you take it. He asked specifically for Jovie. And that would be you."

What the hell ever. Naomi—queen of bullshit.

"Fine, whatever." I make my way toward the back booth. I will myself to have a good attitude. But it's difficult. Really difficult. All I can think about is going home, opening up my laptop, and writing the best damn research paper Dr. Mitchell has ever laid her eyes on. Yeah, right. I really just want to get out of here, go home, and climb in the bed.

"Hi, I'm Jovie. Are you dining alone or will someone else be joining you?" Man, I'm good. I could practically hear a smile in my voice.

The dark-haired guy looks up from his phone. Jack. He smiles and says, "Hey, Jovie. I actually won't be dining at all. I'm just waiting for you to finish your shift."

"Finish my shift? Why?"

"I need you to go somewhere with me. Are you up to it?"

"I don't know. Where?"

"You'll see when we get there. Think of it as a surprise," he says.

"Not a big fan of surprises. I like to know where I'm going before I get there."

This is weird, to say the least. He's like a boomerang. I let go of him, and he always comes back. Sometimes, it's only a few days. Other times, it's a few weeks or a month.

For some reason, I do trust him. I don't think he would do anything to deliberately hurt me. But I also know he can be an asshole. I've seen it firsthand. So why am I even considering this? Hmm... he's pretty irresistible. I hope I won't regret our time together, but for now... I'll just roll with it.

"Just trust me," he says.

I laugh. Not a girly giggle but a deep belly laugh.

"Trust you. Okay, Jack. Whatever you say. Even though, in the short period of time I've known you, you haven't given me one reason to, you know, trust you."

"You're right. I haven't given you a reason, but that's why I'm here. I want to start over. Forget about the first night you met me. Forget about the night I was drunk and the night on the hood of your car—"

"Ahem, forget about..." I mumble

"Well, maybe there are parts about the hood of your car I want to remember, but I definitely want to forget the part where I walked away," he says as his eyes move around the room. Aw, he's acting kind of sweet. Damn him.

"Okay, I'll go, but only because you mentioned the hood of my car."

God, I'm going to pretend I didn't say that out loud. He smiles my favorite lopsided grin.

"How much longer until you can head out?" he asks.

"I can leave now. Let me grab my stuff. Are we going in one

vehicle or do you want me to follow you?"

"Do you mind driving us? It's not too far."

"No. I don't mind. Be back in a few." I turn toward the back of the restaurant and head for the break room.

I hurriedly grab everything from my locker and slam it shut. Wonder what he's up to? Doesn't matter. I have a great attitude tonight. Plus he's being different from usual. In a good way.

"You're not leaving with him, are you?" Naomi. Why does she care?

"Yeah, why? My shift is over unless you need me to do something else before I go."

"No, it's not that at all. You just need to be careful with that one."

"That one? I don't understand."

I slide by her and move closer toward the door.

"Jack. You know who I'm talking about. He's not somebody I think a girl like you needs to hang out with if you know what I mean." She smiles and takes a few steps toward me before continuing. "He doesn't date, ever. Never known him to have one girlfriend. I don't know. You're my friend, and... well, I just don't want to see you get hurt. Especially when you have plenty of other opportunities out there."

"First, I know exactly what I'm getting into with Jack. Nothing. It's not like that."

"Not yet, anyway," she cuts me off.

"Please, Naomi. I know you're my friend and you mean well, but just let me make my own mistakes. I never had that chance growing up. My parents didn't let me do anything. So I never made the wrong decisions or the right ones for that matter. If anything changes, which it won't, I'll be sure to let you know. But for now, just let me hang out with Jack or Ryker or whoever, without making me feel bad or worrying about whether or not I'm doing the right thing."

"Okay, fine. Go have fun. And I promise I won't say I told

you so." She laughs as she turns toward her locker.

"See you tomorrow night."

As I turn the corner making my way back into the dining room, Jack's standing at the bar with that grin. My fucking smile, but he's giving it to someone else. Lena to be exact. She's the big-chested brunette who works here part time but seems to hang out at the bar all of the time. I. Don't. Care.

I approach the two of them. He turns his head and looks at me, still smiling.

"You ready?" he asks.

"Yeah."

He nods toward the front of the restaurant, and we fall into step together. We exit the building through the front door. He reaches into his pocket and pulls out his keys.

"I'm parked on the other side of the building." He motions in the direction of his vehicle.

Once we reach his Jeep, he unlocks the passenger side door before he joins me on the other side. He slides the key in, unlocks my door, and tosses me the keys. What a freaking gentleman.

* * * * *

"It's not too much farther. Just around the corner and to the right."

We have been driving for about twenty minutes outside of town—an area I'm not familiar with. A two lane highway with trees on both sides of the road for miles.

"Slow down. Take a right—here." He points to the road he wants me to take, so I slow down and make the turn. Dirt road. Beginning to feel a little uncomfortable.

"Jack."

"Yeah, we're almost there."

"Will you promise me something?" I quickly glance from the road to Jack and back to the road again.

"No."

I slam on the brakes—the back tires slide from right to left before coming to a complete stop.

"Shit, Jovie. What the hell?"

"I wanna go back. I'm gonna turn around and go back to the restaurant—to my car."

"Wait. Why?"

His lopsided grin is nowhere to be found. Instead, it's replaced with firm lips and raised eyebrows.

"Because, when I asked you if you would promise me something, you said no. Who says no to that question? I've gotten a maybe before, but never a no. Plus the promise I need is a very important one. So, now you know the why." I place my hand on the gearshift to throw it in reverse and get the hell off the creepy dirt road.

"Wait a minute." He puts his hand over mine before continuing. "I don't make promises to anyone. No matter how important the promise is to you. I can't do it. Sorry. That's just the way I am. No promises—ever." He releases my hand.

He's not stopping me from turning around. I haven't known Jack for very long, but he seems to be able to shut down quickly.

"Okay, fine. You win. This dirt road with arching trees is probably beautiful during the day but in the dark, it's freaking creepy. I only wanted you to promise me that you weren't gonna get me out here and chop me into little pieces to feed to the fish. There that's it. Please. Don't. Kill. Me."

He laughs as if it's the funniest thing he's ever heard anyone say. I personally don't think it's funny.

He finally stops laughing and looks at me before saying, "That's the most ridiculous thing I've ever heard. Put the Jeep back in drive and keep going about another mile, then veer to the left."

So I do exactly what he says. I take it slow as I notice the water just ahead. Yeah, fish food. It's so ridiculous, my ass.

"Stop right here and put it in park." I do as he says. Then he hops out and walks around to the driver's side door.

After pulling the door open, he unhooks my seat belt, grabs my hand, and helps me out. Hmm... quite the gentleman... again.

After I'm out, he climbs in behind the steering wheel. Oh, shit. Surely he's not about to leave me. Closing my eyes, I take a deep breath and release it. I do this three more times. When I open my eyes, Jack is standing in front of me.

"What?" I ask.

"Tell me you aren't having one of those episodes."

"Panic attack, Jack. Not an episode. My God, you sound like a—a—ah, well, I don't know, but calling anxiety or panic an episode just sounds uncool."

"That's me. The most uncool person you will ever know. But, hey, being uncool works for me."

"What's that mean?"

"Well, look around." He walks around me slowly until he's made a complete circle. Then he continues, "I'm here at my most favorite, peaceful place in the entire world with the most beautiful chick I've ever had the pleasure to be alone with."

Shit. Damn. Fuck. Why is he being so unlike himself? He's convincing. Very convincing. But I know the truth. It's not really me. It's her. The other blue-eyed girl.

He gently touches the tips of his fingers to mine. No electrical jolt, flash or spark. But it's okay because his touch is so much more than that. Three words—calm—safe—need. Not what I'd expect. Not at all. The tips of his fingers find their way into my hands and he interlocks them with mine. Now he takes my breath away. Without trying. And that is sexy.

"I've backed the Jeep up toward the pond. Come sit with me. I want you to see why this is my favorite place."

He releases my right hand but keeps a tight grip on my left. When we reach the Jeep, he opens the passenger side door and we climb inside. Then he steps over the back seat onto a large built-in box of some kind. I follow closely behind him almost falling before I finally sit down. He opens up the back window so we can get a better view. Even though it's November, the weather is still warm. I sit beside him crossing my legs. The scene in front of me is breathtaking. The moon is full sitting just above a huge tree that somehow has grown in the center of the pond. It's as though the tree was there first and the water flowed in around it. The sounds of nighttime, along with the moon giving off more glow than most inside lights, make this place calming.

"What do you think?" he asks.

"It's great. So peaceful."

"I don't have your anxiety attacks." He holds up both hands and bends his fingers making air quotes.

"Wait a minute… my anxiety attacks? Just so you know anybody can have them, so there not only mine."

He smiles and says, "I know this, but let me finish. Life can sometimes be overwhelming for me even though I'm aware you find that hard to believe. But when it is, this is the place I come to gather my crazy thoughts and put them back where they belong."

"And where is it that your crazy thoughts belong?" I ask.

"Locked away in my mind so tightly that I don't have to worry about them anymore or at least, not for a long time."

"You not driving, I mean—do any of those crazy thoughts have anything to do with the reason you don't drive with someone else in the car?"

"We're not discussing me tonight. Or the reasons I'm the way I am. Just know that I'm me, and I'll be this way until I take my last breath. There is no need for an explanation because it won't change anything, and if I don't talk about it, then it stays locked away in my mind. Now see how simple my mind works?" He laughs and leans into my shoulder giving me a slight nudge.

"Simple—I'm thinking more like complicated. So how did you find this place?"

"It belongs to Stone, you know the guy who owns Southern Stain. I mean the land and the pond both belong to him, but the moon, the stars, and the radiating peaceful vibes all belong to me. I love this place."

"Thank you for bringing me here to your peaceful place in the woods." I look over at his beautiful face. He's looking out toward the tree or the moon or both. The guy here with me tonight isn't the same one I met a few months ago in the locked bathroom. And he's definitely not the same one who walked away from me that night leaving me sitting on the hood of my car.

"I felt like you needed this place. Not sure why, but some people need peace in their life. Don't take this the wrong way, but I think you might be one of those people." He places his hand on my bare leg and squeezes gently. I rest my hand on the top of his. My eyes survey the scenery in front of me once again. This time, I notice the dock that extends out almost to the center. It's just feet away from the tree.

"Can we go there, out on the dock?" I point in the direction of the pond as I glance over toward Jack.

"Yeah, sure."

He hops to his feet and jumps from the built-in box to the ground. The combination of his ass in those jeans with boots and a fitted long sleeve t-shirt are what any girl wants to see standing directly in front of her.

"Jovie?" He's standing in front of me, but I am still lost in thoughts of, well… his ass in those jeans.

"Yeah, sorry." I place my hands in his and move toward the edge. I leap from the back of the Jeep while squeezing his hands tightly. My feet hit the ground with perfect execution.

"You're not cold, are you? I know you didn't know we were going to be outside. And I didn't give you time to change." He's rambling. It's cute. Real damn cute.

"No, I'm good. It's the south, remember. I usually wear shorts to Thanksgiving dinner." I giggle. Giggle? Since when do I giggle? Well… never.

He reaches into the back seat grabbing a small blanket and tucks it under his arm.

"Just in case," he whispers.

We walk down the hill to the dock in silence. He places his left hand on the small of my back to direct me toward the step leading onto the ramp. Once we get to the end, I press my body against the railing and look up at the moon as it glows just over the tree. How in the hell did all of this beauty end up here? In the middle of nowhere? Jack places his hands on either side of me and leans into my back. Holy freaking crap. To hell with the blanket. I shiver slightly before letting the heat from his body consume me. Closing my eyes, I tilt my head back until it's resting on his shoulder, my cheek against his. And there is that smell again. His smell. I wish I could bottle it for later when all of this goes to shit, and I'm alone in my room crying over something I shouldn't have done.

Jack moves his nose to the bend of my neck before he takes in a deep breath and says, "You smell so fucking good."

"You must like greasy beer with a touch of sweat because that's what I smell like after a five-hour shift." I smile as I relax into his touch. His body immediately responds, or at least the lower half of it does. Do I want to do this again? Risk him walking away like last time. Only, this time, he can't walk away because I'm here in the middle of nowhere with no way out.

He chuckles. The sound of his laughter vibrates softly into my neck. I inhale deeply as he moves his hands from the railing to my bare stomach. A chill races over me. He senses it because he pulls me in closer.

"Grease, beer, and sweat are my favorite combination," he whispers.

I move my hands from the railing and wrap them around his wrists. He loosens his grip just enough for me to turn my body until I'm facing him. He lifts his head from my neck. As he stares into my eyes—which concerns me, but I'm gonna let it go—I experience the same thing I did the first night. Calmness. It's not this place. It's him. He has the ability to make me nervous, excited and not to mention, horny. All while giving me freedom from my anxiety.

Jack slides his hands around my waist. The sensation of his fingertips against my bare skin is making me crazy. I move closer to his body until we are touching. My hands go immediately around his neck, and I pull his lips into mine. A soft graze is all I give him. I want more. But I want to be sure he wants more. Nothing more embarrassing than—well, I've been there with him.

"What do you want from me, Jovie," he mumbles, our lips still connected.

I can't answer that question because, honestly, at this moment, I don't want to think or talk. I only want to do. So I slide my hands down his back until I'm able to lift his t-shirt. I tug on it, and within a couple of seconds, it's over his head and lying on the dock. His lips are still so very close to mine. Hovering. Waiting. So I give in to him. To my own want. I press my lips to his. He moans so deeply, the sound is almost more than I can stand. I. Want. Him.

The kiss is slow, soft, and full of desire. He lifts me, and I wrap my legs around his waist. Never losing his balance, he lowers us to the blanket that he somehow had managed to spread out perfectly across the dock. I grind my hips against his erection. The right amount of pressure combined with the friction our bodies create is almost more than I can stand. I have to feel more skin. My skin against his. I quickly unbutton my shirt as our lips separate—reconnect and separate again. I pull my right arm out of the sleeve of my shirt and then shift to remove my left when he pulls his lips from mine and grabs my arm, stopping me from taking off my shirt. *What the hell?* Here we go again. He wants me. He doesn't want me.

He's fucking Ivy and that Halle girl. What's wrong with me? My eyes fill with tears. I'm hurt and embarrassed because I kissed him. I took his shirt off. Me. I started this, only to be shot down—again.

I lower my head because I don't want him to see the emotions that are swimming through my eyes right now. He releases my arm and his hand travels to my face. No. Please. No. As he slowly lifts my chin, tilting my head back, a tear runs down my cheek.

"I want this, Jovie. I'm not stopping it from happening. But there's something I have to tell you before it does."

I manage to hold back the tears. Hoping like hell he didn't see the one that got away.

"Please, don't tell me that you have a disease. Because if that's it, then you're gonna have to count me out." At least, that would make sense. Why he hasn't followed through. And it would make me feel a whole lot better about myself.

"No! I don't have a disease. I can't believe you would even say that out loud. Damn."

"Sorry." I sigh. He leans in kisses my cheek and then laughs softly.

"I want this with you tonight more than I've wanted anything in a long time, but I have to be fair to you. I want you to understand how this has to work. You and I tonight on this dock will fucking rock. But it can never be more. No dating. Because I don't date anybody. It's nothing personal. We can maybe hang out occasionally, but it's only before or after sex. It will never change."

"Wow. Okay. I'm not really sure what I expected you to say, but I understand."

He doesn't explain. He gives no reasons why. Just point blank—we will fuck on his schedule and if I don't agree, then we're done.

He laughs as he moves his hand to my shirt that's still half hanging off my body.

"I assume that's a 'yes, I agree with your terms, Jack. So, you can fuck me now'," he whispers against my skin.

I manage a nod. Then he slides my shirt off and unhooks my bra. My lips are on his chest, then his neck, and finally, his mouth. This kiss is more aggressive. He's not holding anything back. I'm doing this knowing that I'm right back where I was in Brownsboro with Liam. No regrets. This is what I want.

His hands travel... moving much faster than before... more determined to get what he wants. The tips of my fingers move lightly over his skin until I reach the front of his jeans. The button pops open easily. He tugs and twists, lifting the both of us off the dock until he's completely naked—or rather naked down to his knees because those damn boots are halting all progress. Obviously, he's a pro because, within seconds, his boots, pants, and my shorts are all scattered around us.

The light of the moon is now directly over us shining so brightly, I can see every bit of his tattooed skin. So damn gorgeous. Each and every inch of him.

"You're so fucking beautiful," he mumbles as he moves his lips across my jaw and down my neck to my shoulder.

His touch becomes softer. He's taking his time with every deliberate movement. The tension is building with each touch. With each stroke until I can't take it anymore.

"I need you inside of me, now," I moan.

He scrambles for his pants quickly and then hands me a small foil packet. As I scoot back onto his lap, I rip it open. Not my first time, but only the second guy I've ever been intimate with. So the nerves kind of take over. I breathe in deeply before I look down. He's hard. So freaking hard. Oh, God, I'm really doing this. Once the condom is on, Jack lifts me off his lap and slowly lowers me onto his erection. I grind my hips to adjust to his size.

"Okay?" he asks.

Once he's all the way in, my body tenses and then relaxes. I wrap my legs around his waist and meet his every movement.

"Uh-huh," I groan softly.

I throw my head back. His lips find my most sensitive area just below my ear. The combination of his warm breath on my ear and his lips on my skin are driving me crazy. He wraps his arms around my waist pulling me—squeezing me until there is so much friction. Too much. Until I can't take it anymore. My breathing increases until I'm a bit lightheaded—in a good way. Our bodies are so synchronized it seems like we have done this a thousand times. My orgasm finds me starting at my toes. Traveling up my legs until my entire body is tingling. It's teasing me. Then it takes over with one final shiver traveling up my spine. I fall looking into those eyes. His eyes that say more than his voice ever will.

"Oh, Jack," I holler.

His breathing quickens, as his moans grow deeper. He lifts me off and then presses me back down—again, and again, and again until he finds his release.

Immediately, reality sets in. How am I supposed to act? What am I supposed to say? Did I make a mistake? Too late now. Should have run those questions through my mind before having incredible sex under the moonlight with this tattooed god. Now I'm shivering, but I'm not cold.

"You, okay? You're shaking," he says.

"Yeah, I'm good."

Lifting our bodies slightly, he grabs the blanket and pulls it out from under us. He throws it over my shoulders and wraps his arms around me tightly as he burrows his face into my neck. I will my body to stop shivering. This moment is developing into something that's making me uncomfortable. He says only sex, but he's holding me like it's more.

"Thank you," he mumbles into my neck.

"For what?" Please don't say for sex because that would be

downright weird.

"Thank you for understanding my no dating rule. The sex was fucking hot. And as long as we both know going into this how things are gonna work then the hot sex doesn't have to end."

He kisses my neck as he slides out from underneath me. I'm left sitting on the dock wrapped in a blanket wondering. Wondering if I want this type of relationship... again. And wondering who else he has had sex with on the blanket I'm currently wrapped up in. Ewe. I throw it off me as I stand and search for my clothes. He's disposed of the condom and dressed before I can even locate my panties.

"You're welcome, I think."

"You think? What's that supposed to mean?"

"It just feels strange to say you're welcome after sex, Jack. I don't know. But I agree with everything you said. Let's just not say thank you or you're welcome after sex anymore."

"You're right. I will never say thank you after sex again." He laughs.

After I'm completely dressed, he rolls up the blanket, and we head up the hill to the Jeep. As I climb into the driver's seat, I take one last look at the moon hanging low over the pond. Somehow, I know that tonight will more than likely be my only visit to Jack's peaceful oasis.

CHAPTER 18

JACK

"LET'S LEAVE HOUSTON for a while. Maybe a year or so. Just you and me. We can take the time off from school. Travel the east coast and live in little beach towns. Work for a while, and when we get tired of one place, we move on to the next. It'll be fun," Piper says as she pulls herself out of the water and sits next to me on the dock.

She looks so hot in her little black bikini. I'm glad Stone reminded me of this place. Swimming, tanning, and fucking. Not a better combination. Especially when Piper's involved. But she's always up for fucking no matter where we are.

"You know I would do it, but my dad would shit himself. He has me on a plan, and according to him, I can't alter it at all. You know he doesn't really even like me working. Especially not at Southern Stain."

"My parents won't be thrilled either, but if we both work, then we won't need their money."

"It's not the money, Piper. It's just I promised my dad I would finish school within a reasonable amount of time, so I can go back home and work with him at the firm. He's not bringing anybody new in because he's counting on me."

She swings her leg over my lap and straddles me. Her wet bikini bottoms are so thin I can feel her heat. Her teeth find my earlobe, and she gives it a gentle pull.

"Come on, Jack. Just you and me. I need you to take me away. I want this. You won't regret it," she whispers.

"Give me a little time. Let me see if I can even do it without facing the wrath of my dad."

I'll never be able to explain this one to dear ole dad. He's a rule follower and therefore, expects everyone else to be. He sent me to school to graduate with a degree in accounting, become a CPA, and take over his precious firm. Never veer from the course. My entire life. Becoming a tattoo artist and working at Southern Stain have been my only choices. And he's not happy about either one, but he allowed it because I'm still on course. Now Piper is about to shred dad's dreams to pieces.

"Okay. I can do that." She winks before she slides off me and jumps back into the pond.

"Come in, Jack. The water is great. It'll be better once you're in here with me."

I dive in and swim out to her. We make our way to the small island in the center with the fucking huge ass tree. How in the hell this happened, I'll never know. But it does give the place character. She falls to the ground on her back. I hover over her kissing every inch of her skin I can reach with my lips. She wiggles underneath me. She's so damn ticklish.

"What's wrong, Piper," I ask between kisses.

"Please, Jack, you're—" She's laughing.

I alternate licking and kissing while sliding my hands up and down her bare skin. She breaks free and backs up against the tree.

"That's enough," she screeches

"I'm just getting started." I move in closer so she knows I'm not done.

"No more kisses. No more licks. Fuck me, Jack. And then take me home. I have a meeting tonight."

"You know I want to but no condom."

"You don't need one. We've been over this a thousand times. I'm on the pill."

"And a thousand times I've told you... no condom... no fucking. But the good news is. I have a box of condoms in the truck, so let's get the hell off this island."

She dives in first and I follow behind. She reaches the dock, pulls herself up, slips on her shoes, and runs for the truck. By the time I get there, she's dressed and sitting in the passenger's seat looking at her phone.

"What the hell. I expected you to be naked and waiting in the back of the truck."

"You should have taken advantage when you had the chance. The mood's passed and I have a meeting. So you can take me home now."

Sometimes I think there is something seriously wrong with this chick. One minute, wide open and the next minute, quiet and reserved.

"Yeah, okay. Do you want me to take you to your meeting tonight?"

"You know I like to go to the meetings alone. It would make me too uncomfortable to have you there. I love you, Jack. But my family problems are mine, and I only share them in the group because everyone else there suffers from the same issues. I don't want to drag someone in who wouldn't understand. You know what I mean?"

"Sure, Piper. I understand that you want me to give up my life to travel across the country with you, but yet you don't even want me to go with you to an Ala-non meeting. But it's cool."

"I'm so glad you understand. My family is a complete mess. Maybe one day you'll have the opportunity to see for yourself. But until then, I think it's best if it's just you and me without any family."

So I do as I'm told—crank the truck, throw it in drive, and take her home.

CHAPTER 19

JOVIE

"I'M SO HAPPY you decided to not spend Thanksgiving alone. Today is perfect. I have so much to be thankful for. You—my best friend, and Sebastian—my boyfriend." Layla giggles.

I look out the car window and notice the leaves are finally showing their true fall colors. I love fall.

"Did I tell you Ryker texted me last week?" I ask.

"No, what about?"

"About today. He invited me to Thanksgiving dinner too. I guess maybe Sebastian told him what I said about not wanting to impose or whatever, so I'm sure he's only being nice."

"I call bullshit, Jovie. No guy is just nice. They all have motives. You know that. And most of the time it involves you getting naked. Speaking of getting naked—heard any more from Mr. One Night Stand?"

"Who?"

"You know who I'm talking about. The hot, tattooed god. Well, that's how you referred to him when you told me about the night on the dock."

"Oh—you mean Jack. Nope, not a word."

At least, that's what I want her to think. She doesn't need to know I've crawled into his bed every night since. According to his rules, me being at his place is kind of a no-go, but I assume he's

106

allowing it because of my living situation. I told him, I didn't want Layla to know. It's not her business. So it's our little secret. His and mine. Nobody else needs to know.

"You don't think it's strange?"

"What's strange about it, Layla?"

"That he hasn't called or texted or made any contact. I thought you said he wanted to hook up and hang out, just not date."

"No. What I said is that he wants to fuck. And not date. You must have misunderstood me."

"Don't let him do that to you, Jovie. It's not right. You're too good to let him use you."

"He's not using me. Please, Layla, can we not argue about this today? I swear you and Naomi. She says the same shit. It's Thanksgiving. I purposely didn't go home because I wanted a bitch free day, so don't make me regret staying."

She turns onto a narrow road that looks like it may be the driveway. One can hope. Because I'm ready to get out of this car.

"Sorry, Jovie. You know I love you. Just watching out for my best friend."

"I get it, but I'll tell you just like I told Naomi. I've got to make my own mistakes and move on. Not saying that Jack is or was a mistake, but still—just let me deal with it."

She pulls up into the yard. Yes, the yard. Because the circular driveway is completely full. And there are already several cars parked on the grass, so I guess we're okay. The place is packed.

The house is dark brick with a huge wrap around porch. Very warm and inviting. The front door opens and a tall brown-haired guy walks out onto the porch. Sebastian.

"So? I texted him to come get us. You know I don't like to feel awkward. And us walking into the unknown would be… well, awkward," Layla says as she shrugs and opens her door.

She squeals, giggles, and then jumps into Sebastian's arms. They kiss and kiss and kiss. Damn them. I should have stayed home, made cheese dip, and watched the Macy's Day parade. My phone vibrates in my purse, which, thankfully, pulls me away from watching the rubdown going on just outside my window. I grab it from my open bag. The smile that finds my face is unavoidable. Smiling at the sight of his text is so juvenile, but I love the way it makes me feel to know he is thinking about me at this very minute. Hell, it's Thanksgiving. I have no idea where he is or who he's with, but at this moment, it's me—at least, in his thoughts. I slide my finger across the screen and punch in the code to reveal my message.

Him: Meet me at my place tonight. There's something I want you to see.

Me: I thought that's what I've been doing every night for… well, every night.

Him: You have, but there's a painting I just finished this morning, and I want you to be the first to see it.

Me: Can't wait.

And those two little one-line messages just made my day. After tossing my phone back into my bag, I open the door and exit the car. Wet sloppy kissing and moaning are two sounds I prefer not to hear. Unfortunately, it's the torture my ears are met with as I walk away from the car.

"Would you guys stop it? If you're gonna fuck, just get back in the car and do it already. Because what you're doing out here in the open for everyone to see is disgusting."

"Jovie!" Layla yells.

"Really, Layla. Let's either go inside or leave. I mean, don't you guys do it every day, anyway?" I raise my hand in front of my face before continuing, "Oh, wait. Yes, you do, because I listen to it every night from across the hall. Ugh!"

"Hi, Jovie. Sorry you have to experience our fucking on a daily basis. Maybe we need to go back to my place more often and share the experience with my roommates." He throws his head back and laughs.

Yeah, he thinks I'm kidding, but trust me I'm not. Sometimes guys are so gross. Except for Jack. He's not gross. Ever.

We head for the front door, Sebastian still laughing and Layla grinning from ear to ear. And me, well, I just want this day to end so I can see Jack. Before we make it inside, Ryker is standing in front of the doorway. He's really cute. Sandy blond hair that falls just below his eyebrows. Blue eyes with freckles scattered over his fair skin. And one small dimple in each cheek. His boyish grin gives off the vibe that all is right in the world. Luckily, today that's true. At least in my world.

"Jovie, glad you're here."

"Thanks for inviting me. I guess I didn't realize you guys have such a big family."

"Yeah, holidays are always crazy. Y'all come inside. We're about to sit down for lunch."

He reaches for my hand and immediately, guilt sweeps over me. Jack isn't my boyfriend. I'm not doing anything wrong, but I don't like feeling as if I am.

Layla and I drop our bags off in the hallway before following the guys into the dining room. There are people everywhere. A baby crying, kids running around and around the large table, and some old guy in the corner smoking a cigar. This is great. Nothing like a huge family to make it easy to blend in. I like blending in.

Ryker and Sebastian introduce us, but no one is paying any attention. They are too involved in their own conversation. Not counting, I would guess twenty-five people, maybe thirty. Ryker points me in the direction of our chairs and Layla follows Sebastian to the opposite side.

"What do you think?" Ryker asks.

"It's great. At home, it's only my mom and dad and me. And holidays are just regular days. So I think you're lucky to have all these people." I smile as I sit down next to him.

My eyes move from right to left, examining every single person at the table. Then I make my way back to the person sitting directly in front of me. Shit. Ivy. I mean, I know she's Ryker's sister, but I completely forgot about her being here. She has a look on her face like she can't wait to say something mean. What a bitch. I'm sure she's the reason her brother doesn't have a girlfriend. Nobody wants to put up with her. Well, except maybe Jack. *Don't think about it, Jovie.* He's not here with her. Hell, he's not with me either.

"Hmmm… did you ask Mom before you brought the slut home for Thanksgiving?"

She looks from me to Ryker and then back to me. She knows. Somehow, she found out I've been sleeping with Jack. She's right. Maybe I am a slut. But what does that make her?

"Not today, Ivy. Not today. It's Thanksgiving, and Jovie is here with me. So don't start your evil shit, or I will embarrass you in front of everybody. And you know I can," he says.

He leans in toward me, whispering, "Just ignore her. She's a bitch. She can't help it. She was born that way. Plus she's mad because Jack didn't show up. So she's taking it out on everybody else."

"I understand," I mumble.

I glance back at Ivy's glowering face and smile. Why? Mostly because she's a bitch. But more importantly because Jack didn't show.

Lunch is uneventful. Ryker is sweet. He includes me in conversations, introduces me to his parents, and defends me each time Ivy throws an insult my way.

After lunch, he gives me a tour of the house. I learn that this is actually his family's home where he grew up. We make our way upstairs for the final leg of the tour that happens to end in his former bedroom. Of course, it does. He opens the door, and I am surrounded by all things Ryker. Two electric guitars lean against the bay window. A huge wooden-framed bed with sheets of music scattered all over the mattress. A drum set sits in the center of the room, and some type of surround sound system in the back corner with four speakers placed in different locations in the room. This room is perfect. And even though I don't know him well, I'm positive this room screams Ryker Cole.

"Your dad looks good. Is he feeling better? You know, from the night of the gallery crawl when he had to go to the hospital."

I didn't want to mention anything at dinner because I don't know what's wrong with him. Since his dad and mom were so welcoming and friendly, choosing my words carefully was a top priority.

"Yeah, he's much better. He was in a fire as a kid and it caused him to have permanent lung problems. But he has also smoked for twenty years too, so that doesn't help either. But he's good now," he says as he closes the door.

I walk over to the bay window overlooking the backyard. My heart's racing and my stomach's churning. Not anxiety. Genuine nerves. No butterflies or sweaty palms, but fear that Ryker wants more. And I'm afraid more is gonna be in this room on his bed. I can't do it. I just can't.

His touch is gentle as he turns my body slightly until I'm facing him. Blue eyes are all I can focus on.

"What do you think?" he whispers before he moves his hand to my face.

"What do I think about—" I can't finish because, in a split second, his lips are on mine. And it's not so bad. It's actually not bad at all.

His lips are soft, gentle like his touch. My eyes drift shut as I skim my fingers up his chest and around his neck. He backs me up until I'm pressed against the window. His hand moves from my face, slides down my arm and waist until he grips my leg. Lifting it, he wraps my leg around his waist and presses his erection into my— *Holy shit.*

I wiggle trying to free myself from his hold. But he

apparently thinks I'm squirming for a different reason. He presses against me harder as his hand finds my ass. He grips it tight, so tight it feels like his fingers are touching my bare skin. His mouth moves from my lips to my chin and along my jaw toward my ear. Heavy breathing becomes moaning just as his lips find my ear. All of his movements are smooth, as though each is carefully planned. As if he plotted to get what he wants. The rubbing, grinding and moaning are causing me to lose it. My mind is giving into my raging lust.

Jack. He is all I can see behind my closed eyes. I tell myself that I don't care if he's fucking Ivy or whoever the hell else. I'm not doing this with Ryker, so I grasp his arms and push him away. He moves without hesitation. Those blue eyes are now dark with desire, and I'm sorry that I let it go this far.

"I can't do this. I'm sorry if I led you to think differently," I whisper.

Staring into my eyes before he leans in and places a kiss on my cheek, he mumbles, "It's because of him, isn't it?"

I swallow hard. Take a deep and focus on the question. Him? Hmmm...

"Him?" I ask.

"Yes, Jovie. Him. As in Jack. The reason you won't do this is because of Jack, isn't it?"

"Why would you think that? I mean what would make you ask me such a crazy question?"

He laughs—then moves in a little closer—again.

"Everybody knows. It's not a secret. I just want you to admit it," he says.

"Look, Ryker. I like you. I mean this—what we just did was borderline amazing. But I'm not that kind of girl. We've been on one date. And today has been great, but still. It's too soon for me to have sex with you." I'm a terrible liar. I rub the side of my face before tucking a piece of hair behind my ear. See—I'm getting fidgety. This is what I do when I don't tell the truth. I want to scream, *yes, it's because of him.* But I can't. At least not at this point, anyway.

"I understand. But I want you to know that I think you're pretty great. And beautiful. Did I mention how beautiful you are?"

The blood rushes to my face. It's flushing—I'm sure a bright red. I look down toward my feet so he doesn't notice. But he quickly places his finger under my chin and lifts my face to where looking into his eyes is unavoidable.

"Please be careful with him. Jack's my friend. He's had this thing with my sister off and on for a few years. But he has issues. And his problems run deep. You deserve so much more than what he's got to offer you." He kisses me lightly on the forehead before continuing. "He's not gonna take you out and treat you the way you deserve. He'll keep you around as long as you don't become too attached. And when you do, he'll walk away and never look back."

"Thanks for the warning," falls from my mouth. What's up with everybody protecting me from Jack? Is he really that bad? Poor guy. I actually feel sorry for him.

I move around Ryker, leaving him leaning against the window.

As I reach the door, he says, "I want to take you out. Spend time with you. That's what I have to offer. And the other, yeah, I want that too. But I'd never hide you from the world. Keep you around just to fuck and then do the same with three or four others at the same time. You deserve to be the only one, not one of four."

My eyes fill with tears as I open the door and walk across the hall to the bathroom. As I reach for the knob to the door, it opens. Damn it. Pale green eyes looking directly into my blue ones. A smirk follows before the words begin to roll off her tongue.

"Remember the first night we met? At Jake's bar?" Ivy asks.

"Yeah, why?"

"Obviously, you don't, because I told you that night to stay away from my brother. You didn't listen—"

"No, you didn't tell me to stay away. As I recall, you said he wasn't interested, which is completely untrue—because, as you can see, he is."

"I'm telling you this now… stay away from my brother. He has plenty of groupie sluts to choose from, and he doesn't need another one."

"I'm not going to stand here and argue with you about your brother. I'm not interested in anything more than friendship. So don't worry yourself about me."

Forget the bathroom. My tears have dried and steam is rising from the top of my head. I've got to get the hell away from this crazy bitch before I say more than I should. I walk down the hall, and just as I reach the staircase, she spews her evil confession so loudly that everyone in this house now knows the truth.

"I know you're fucking Jack."

I stop in my tracks. I'm paralyzed. Numbness from my feet shooting up my legs to my waist. No feeling at all. Then she's behind me. Her perfume is strong, bold, a smell that causes my throat to tickle.

Her body is inches from mine as she bends down near my ear and says, "He told me last night as I rode his dick so fucking hard. I promised him the release that he so desperately wanted for the truth. I bet you don't have that kind of control over him. Do you? No truth. No orgasm. Plain and simple. So he gave me what I asked for… the truth. And then I was kind enough to let him fill me with his release."

I suddenly need to cough, to cry… to run and hide. No, not because of anxiety, but because of hurt. He fucked me last night. Did he sleep with her first? I can't even think about it anymore. She's a cruel bitch, but I'm afraid I'll cry if I continue this conversation with her. And the last thing I want is for her to see me cry.

"Ivy! Leave her the fuck alone. I warned you."

It's Ryker. He's trying to look out for me. If for no other reason, because of Ivy, I could never be in a relationship with Ryker. She would destroy me. I'm just not that strong. My feet and legs regain feeling so I take a few steps toward the stairs. She's still not done. She just can't let it go.

"I hope you haven't fucked her, my dear sweet brother. Because you know she's been fucking Jack and God knows who else." She lets out a cackle. God, such an irritating laugh. But so appropriate for her. I continue down the stairs leaving them to finish the conversation that I no longer want any part of. As soon as I find Layla, we head outside toward the car. I fall into the passenger's seat and cry.

CHAPTER 20

JACK

SHE'S STANDING AT my front door at seven o'clock just like she promised. Beautiful, but with an air of sadness. Swollen red eyes and flushed cheeks greet me as she walks into my condo. I didn't think she would show. Ryker called me about two hours ago and filled me in on today's Thanksgiving fiasco.

"I'm glad you came," I say as I reach for her hand. She pulls back like holding my hand is the last thing she wants to do tonight.

"I said I would, so I'm here. You have something to show me?"

She's not happy with me. Not at all.

"Yeah, it's in the studio."

"Studio?" Her eyebrows rise as her eyes dart around the room.

She's confused. And it's fucking adorable. I've never shown her my art. It's mostly private. Only for me, but now that I took a leap out into the art world, I'm loosening up some. What little bit of exposure I got that night from my first showing gave me just enough confidence to branch out. Design things out of my comfort zone. Comfort zone meaning people and faces. Now, I want to show the world I can do more. So much more.

"I converted the basement into a small studio. It's where I draw—design the art for Southern Stain. It's also, where I paint. You know like the art from my showing."

"Oh," is all that tumbles from her perfect lips.

"Follow me," I reach for her hand again, but she steps away.

I don't know what she wants. She shows up here tonight, but yet she's distant. Very non-Jovie. I hate to be a dick, but she knew what she was getting into from the beginning. And now, here we are at what I assume to be the end, and she's acting like a damn girlfriend.

We walk down the narrow staircase. Once she steps off the last step, her face lights up. She moves slowly toward the wall and takes in every painting. Every sketch.

"It's over here."

"What?" She turns away from the wall to face me.

"The painting. The one I want you to see."

She walks toward me, and when she sees the oversized canvas, her lips curl up into a breath-taking smile.

Walking away from her isn't going to be easy. The feelings I have let myself develop over the last few weeks are borderline pathetic. I know I shouldn't have fucked her in my bed—mistake number one. Mistake number two—every night. In my bed every night. What the hell is wrong with me? I let my constant need to protect her override every rational bone in my body. And the sex. Well, fucking unbelievable doesn't give it justice.

"Jack, it's beautiful. You're talented. I mean really good," she says.

"I couldn't stop thinking about that night. That place is so damn peaceful. I decided to paint it."

"I love it. The dock, the water, with the tree and the moon. It's perfect. Thank you."

"For what?"

"For showing me this painting. I know how private you are about certain things. Well, pretty much everything. But you took me to this place and now you're letting me see it again—through your eyes. So, thank you." She smiles as her fingers move along the border of the canvas.

Why does she have to be so fucking perfect? These types of thoughts will get me in trouble. Make me think I want more than I actually do. Even if I'm willing to overlook a rule or two, it will never work. Because it can't. I won't allow it long term. So I'm about to do this now rather than later. To be honest, it's gonna suck.

"I know what happened at the Cole's today," I say.

"No, Jack. You don't know what happened today. The only thing you know is what someone else told you. And I assume that someone was Ivy."

"It doesn't matter how I know or who told me. What matters is that this thing we have is becoming complicated. And I don't do complicated."

She steps away from the painting and looks directly into my eyes.

"It's only complicated if you allow it to be. But what happened today at the Cole's was nothing short of humiliating. And I refuse to continue whatever this rule induced fuck buddy system you have going here with multiple females. It's just not for me."

She takes one last look at the painting and then returns her eyes to mine.

"I feel sorry for you, Jack. You really need to work on fixing whatever it is that's broken in your life. You have a beautiful soul. I've seen it in just this short period of time we've been together. You deserve to be happy. Hell, happiness is something we all deserve. I wish you luck in finding it."

She brings her hand to my cheek, stands on her toes, and leans in and kisses my lips softly. Then she turns around—walks upstairs. The front door opens and closes. I do nothing. No movement. I just let the best thing in my life walk away without as much as a goodbye.

CHAPTER 21

JOVIE

"I HAVEN'T HAD any anxiety or panic in close to a month now. So I'm fixed—cured. Right?" I ask Dr. Birch. These meetings are getting kinda old. Same shit, different day.

"Are you still taking your medication?"

"No. Remember, I told you I'm not going to take that medicine. I don't need it. I refuse to rely on a pill to fix my problems."

She smiles and types some bullshit into her laptop. I'm sure she's reminding herself of how stubborn I am. And how I don't follow the protocol like the rest of her anxiety-stricken patients do.

"Jovie, you of all people should know how anxiety works. You'll be fine for a while and then it's back. I just want you to realize this before you ultimately decide against taking the medication."

"Yes, I do realize that, but I'm just not ready to become a zombie. I want to enjoy life."

"Is that what you're doing now? Enjoying life?" She straightens her skirt as she uncrosses her legs. Her eyes follow the movement of my head as I look around the room.

"Yes, of course, I'm enjoying life. Isn't that what all nineteen-year-old college students do?"

"Are you still seeing that guy? Hmmm…" she's searching her screen looking for the identity of the person she thinks is the source of my happiness, but hopefully, she won't find it. I don't even want to hear the sound of his name.

"It's Jack, isn't it? Are you still seeing him?" She smiles.

"No, I'm not. It was never like that. I tried to explain that last week. We were friends and now we're not. And I would rather not discuss him today. This session is about me, not him."

I'm snappy and rude. Two things that are not me. I didn't tell her about Ivy, Ryker, and Thanksgiving. And I certainly didn't tell her that I walked out of Jack's life two weeks ago without looking back. But what really sucks is that he didn't try to stop me. He hasn't called or texted. No communication. So, I guess everything I've heard about him is true. When he's done… well, he's done. I meant nothing to him. All lies about wanting to protect me from my anxiety. To help me find my peaceful place was a ploy to get me into his bed every night. And it worked.

"Jovie, I know there's more to this story, but I'm not going to pry. I'll give you your privacy, but if it causes you to have an increase in your anxiety, then we'll have to discuss it."

"I told you my anxiety is better, much better. I just really want to focus on school right now. I feel like it is the one thing that is giving me some direction."

She looks down at her watch before saying, "We don't have but about ten minutes left. I want to mention one other topic that I know you don't want to discuss, but it's important."

I know what topic it is. My dead sister. The cemetery, the fainting, and the hospital. I don't want to discuss it. Not today and not ever. I will never go back to that gravesite again. Never.

Standing quickly from the couch, I scan the room like a trapped animal looking for my escape. I'm sure she knows that I want out. She's a smart lady. Sometimes too damn smart.

"What are you doing?" she asks.

"I'm leaving. I forgot that I have to go into work early. So I need to head out so I can change."

"Jovie. I understand you don't want to discuss what

happened that day at the gravesite. I've tried to give you some time to heal. But you can't bury it away. It's only a source of more problems further down the road."

I nod and then shrug my shoulders as if I don't care. Because honestly, at this point, I don't.

"I understand, Dr. Birch. But today has been tiring. And then to come here and discuss Jack, the gravesite, and my dead sister. Well, it's just too much. Can we please save it for next week? I promise I'll be ready and willing to talk about anything you think we need to discuss."

I shuffle away from the couch toward the door, hoping to be free before she replies to my last comment.

But as luck would have it, I barely make it to the back of the couch before I hear her flat voice say, "I'm making a note of that. Anything I feel important will be discussed next week. Done. So, you better be ready to do some serious discussing then."

She stands and follows me to the door. I push it open and walk out into the empty lobby. She places her hand on my shoulder and squeezes gently.

"I'm on your side, Jovie. I want you to get everything out of life that you want and deserve. But sometimes, it takes a lot of work to get there. I promise I'm willing to put forth the effort to see this through. I just hope you feel the same way."

I want to tell her that I do, but I'm done for today. No more discussing my issues and the tragedies that led me to this particular point in my life.

"Bye, Dr. Birch. See you next week."

I walk across the lobby and through the exit door. The sun greets me as the cool breeze blows my hair across my face. This is my life and I refuse to let any harboring emotions control it. I head for my car leaving all thoughts of my meeting with Dr. Birch behind me.

CHAPTER 22

Seven years and one month earlier

Jack

"SO, WHAT DO you think?" I look over at Annie as she flips through my sketchbook.

"Is this sketch new? I may want you to put this design on my shoulder," she says.

I lean over and look at the sketch. It's so simple but perfect for the shoulder. Especially for someone as small as Annie. It's a half heart with an infinity symbol through the bottom. I call it forever love. Kinda corny, but chicks fall all over that shit.

"No, it's not new. You know I'll do whatever design you want, but you just completely ignored my question."

She shrugs and closes the sketchbook. Then she taps her fingers over and over again on the counter. Something's going on. I know her too well. She's shitty at hiding her feelings.

"I don't remember the question. I wasn't paying attention."

"You were paying attention but decided to ignore the question. Come on, Annie. I know you better than that. At least, give me some credit."

"Okay, then no. No, I don't think you should take a year off school to run all over the country with Piper. It's a bad idea."

"See, now that wasn't so hard, was it? But my mind is made up. I'm doing it. I love her, and if she wants to travel, then I'm going with her. We can finish school anytime."

"Do you plan on finishing this semester or are you just gonna up and leave now. It's only September. What's three more months?"

"Probably finish this semester. It's paid for. And Thomas Alexander is gonna be fucking livid as it is. So I'm sure not gonna piss away a semester he's already paid for."

Annie scoots over closer to me. She nudges me slightly with her shoulder. I glance at her. Her head hangs down and her dark hair is covering her face.

"You need to stop with the hints. Fucking tell me what's up."

"I'm not hinting at anything."

"I call bullshit. You're acting all strange and shit. Not paying attention to anything I say. Avoiding my questions. Now tell me."

She lifts her head as she turns to face me. She forces a smile before she lets the words flow.

"Just remember that you asked for this. And when I'm done, I want you to know that I was gonna tell you. It just wasn't going to be today. Because believe it or not—I love you. You are my best friend. My family. I've known you my entire life. And I never want to hurt you, but I couldn't live with myself if I just stood by and let this happen." She takes in a deep breath and closes her eyes.

"Just fucking say it, Annie. I'm a big boy. Are you pregnant? Because, if you are, I'm gonna beat Bennett's ass."

Her eyes grow wide before she throws her head back and laughs.

"No, I'm not pregnant. What gave you that dumbass idea?"

"You. I've never seen you act like this. So I figured it must be hormones or some female shit. Now finish."

"Okay. Look, the other night at my meeting, I forgot my bag in the car. Sally had already started so I went out the side door, which meant I had to walk half the building to get around to the front. As I rounded the side corner, I saw her with him, so my nosey ass hung back to see what was going on. Maybe it's nothing. A couple of friends running into each other. You know, innocent. But Jack, it wasn't—"

"What in the fuck are you talking about? Her and him. Innocent. You have lost your mind, right?"

"See, I'm terrible at this shit. I can't hurt you, Jack. I just can't."

I know she's talking about Piper. Because she has meetings the same night. I know her, but now she has to tell me. She fucking has to.

"I'll make this a little easier for you. The 'her' you're talking about is Piper. Am I right?" I ask.

Tears fill her eyes and she looks away.

"Annie, you have to tell me. Please." I'm not begging, but at this point, it is an option.

"Fuck it. I saw Piper outside the church last week with… Caleb. I'm sorry, Jack. I had to tell you. I couldn't let you throw your life away over some slut."

"Slut? Did you see them fucking? If not, you have no right to talk about her like that. Just because she was standing outside the church with Caleb doesn't mean anything. I'm sure they have a good reason."

Tears roll down her cheeks. Her breathing picks up as she takes in a deep breath.

"A good reason. What the hell is wrong with you, Jack? She fucking kissed him outside the passenger side door for at least five minutes before she crawled inside the car. And then they left. She kissed him and left with him. Did she stay at your place last Thursday night? Answer that question." She's screaming—at me. Anger spews out with every word. She wants me to believe what she thinks she saw. But last Thursday night Piper showed up at my place drunk. Took a shower and went straight to sleep.

"Yes, she did stay at my place last Thursday. Are you sure it was Piper? Maybe you're mistaken."

"What the fuck ever, Jack. Believe she's not fucking Caleb. I don't care. The truth will come out and when it does, I'll even be kind enough not to say I told you so. I don't trust him at all. He's a male whore. And your girlfriend. Well, she's the female equivalent."

"That's enough, Annie. We don't know that anything happened. Just let me talk to Piper about it."

"No, you can't. Trust me. Wait and watch. You'll see it for yourself," she pleads.

"So I'm supposed to just ignore what you told me. Sit around and wait for her to do something wrong. Like, fuck my friend."

"Yes. That's exactly what you've gotta do. If you ask her, she won't admit it. I mean if you were fucking around, would you?"

"I wouldn't be fucking around. That's not me. And she's never given me any indication—"

"Come on, Jack. Watch her—pay attention. I mean I hope it's not true, but if it is, you need to let her go. I can't stand the thought of her fucking that asshole. And then he hangs out with you like nothing's going on."

She wraps her arms around my neck. Her tears are warm on my cheek as she squeezes me tightly.

"I believe you, Annie. It's just hard. I really do love her. Next month, it'll be a year that we've been together. I guess I'm naïve or dumb because I thought I could trust her."

"I know. And I hope it's not true. But if it is, remember I'm here for you."

The door to the shop opens, Annie jumps back, and I turn toward the lobby to greet the customer. Only it's not a client.

"Hey, guys. Did I interrupt something?" Caleb laughs as he looks between Annie and me before continuing. "I can leave—come back later if you want to be alone. I think my first client isn't for another hour."

I clench my fist while moving away from Annie. I will myself to keep my mouth shut, but Annie can't do it. She turns so she is facing him dead center. She pauses a beat before rolling her eyes.

"Fuck you, Caleb." She turns, throws up her middle finger, and walks toward the back.

"Didn't we try that once before? Yeah, I think we did. And it didn't work out, did it?"

She completely ignores him. After walking into her station, she slams her door so hard the damn wall shakes.

I look over at Caleb and he's staring back—grinning like the asshole he is.

"What? She didn't tell you we fucked?" He laughs and laughs, and fucking continues to laugh—I suddenly want to punch him in the mouth. Maybe then he would stop the fucking laughter.

I want to run inside Annie's station and shake the shit out of her. She fucked him. Now he's probably fucking my girlfriend. My best friend and my girlfriend. I walk away before I wrap my hands around his neck and choke him within inches of his sad life. As I make my way down the hall, the sound of his words plays over and over in my mind.

CHAPTER 23

PRESENT DAY

JOVIE

"ARE YOU EXCITED about band night?" Layla asks as we walk in the employee entrance of Overtime.

"Yeah, I guess. We'll be busier, which means better tips. Oh, and more roaming hands." I snicker.

Not something I'm looking forward to—the worst part of this job is the drunken guys with hands they can't seem to control. But, honestly, I don't think it bothers Layla or Naomi. Because I seem to be the only one who ever complains about it.

"That's not really what I meant, but you're right. Tips will be better tonight because I bet the place is gonna be packed," she squeals.

"What did you really mean, Layla? Please stop trying to protect me. I'm fine. Really. Therapy is going great. No more anxiety attacks. And it's been weeks since I last talked to Jack. Christmas is around the corner, so I'm really good. I promise."

Layla stops mid-step and faces me. She leans over, wraps one arm around my shoulder pulling me in for a quick hug.

"I love you, girlie. Have since we were twelve. It's not Jack I'm worried about. It's Ivy. I know you haven't seen her since Thanksgiving. Just want you to be prepared in case she's being her usual self."

"You mean queen of the mean girls? Yeah, I'm ready for her." I giggle as we continue our journey inside.

Why did Nocturnal Revolution have to be the first band to play on band night? It's great that management has decided to branch out. Having local bands playing once a week is a great idea, but Ivy here—tonight. I guess I'll just deal with it. Plus she'll probably be fine with me now that she has Jack all to herself. And since Ryker and I aren't actually hanging out. So she has no reason to spew her venom my way.

"Don't look now, but Jack just walked through the door," Naomi says.

"Who's he with?"

Shit. Why did I ask that? Now it looks like I care. I mean I do care, but that's my business. Not for anyone else to know.

"Stone, Annie, and Fish. Everybody from Southern Stain. Did you know he was coming?"

"How would I know? Haven't seen or spoken to Jack in weeks. I should be asking you the same question. I mean, aren't you and Stone kind of seeing each other?"

"Absolutely not. We hang out sometimes, but mostly, we just have sex. He's a whore. Sleeps with a different girl every night. I would never date somebody like that." She laughs.

I'm not even going to respond to that statement. I thought I had relationship issues. But it's clear I'm not alone.

"Oh, good. They put them in your section. Thank God," I say to Naomi.

She heads toward their table, and I move toward the bar to pick up my drink order. I avoid looking at the stage because I know my eyes won't be able to avoid her. It's human nature to want to look at the things you shouldn't. And I shouldn't want to look at her. Who cares if she's watching Jack and he's watching her. I don't.

The band has been on about an hour. So far, everything is good. The place is packed. Layla's off tonight, so she's hanging out near the stage drooling. My shift ends in about thirty minutes. So, if all goes well, I can get out of here without crossing paths with anybody who is gonna cause me grief.

"Hey, can you do me a favor?" Naomi asks as I move around her heading toward the kitchen.

"Sure, whatcha need?"

"Drop these drinks off at table number six. I've got to pee. Like really bad."

I look over my shoulder. Table number six. Nope, not Jack's table—three over, so yep, I'll do it.

Grabbing her tray, I head for the other side of the restaurant.

Three guys in their late twenties greet me as I serve their drinks.

"So, did you take over for Naomi?" the blond asks.

"Nope, just bringing out this round of drinks for her. You guys need anything else."

"Yeah, you in the bathroom, on your knees, with my dick in your mouth," says the dark-haired guy closest to me.

His friends choke out a laugh, but all eyes remain on me. Waiting for my reaction. Well, they're not getting one. I know better than to encourage the drunk. I turn to walk away when a hand grabs my bare leg and pulls me back. I lose my balance and fall into the lap of the disgusting asshole who offered me his dick.

"Okay, guys. Not funny. Let me up," I shriek.

This guy is pissing me off. Not only did he pull me into his lap, but now he's wrapped his arm around my waist pressing my ass into his erection. Do guys really think this type of behavior will make a girl want to have sex?

"You feel that? Meet me in the bathroom, and I'll let you ride it." He points toward the back hall where the bathroom is located.

Okay. Now he's gone too far. I'm tempted to hit him over the head with my serving tray, but I'm scared I might kill him. And I certainly don't want to go to jail tonight.

"Let me up. I mean it," I yell.

"Let go of her, now."

Ryker is standing in front of me. His fair skin is flushed and his blue eyes dark. He's pissed. I glance at the stage. No band. I didn't even realize they were done. That's how long I've been at this table. Fucking assholes.

"Does she belong to you?" the dark haired guy asks.

"No, but she belongs to me. Let. Her. Go."

Jack. Where the hell did he come from? Wait a minute—I don't belong to him. I look at Jack then at Ryker and over my shoulder at the jerk who just won't give up. He blows his ragged breath onto my neck before he lets out a deep grumble.

"Do you belong to this asshole, sweetheart?"

"That seems to be the million dollar question. Doesn't it?" Ivy wails.

Where the fuck did she come from? Now my problem has turned into a freaking three-ringed circus with Ivy as the ringmaster.

Jack grabs my arm and pulls me off the guy.

"Are you okay?" he asks.

"Yeah, I'm good. Thanks."

"Keep your fucking hands off her. Understand?" Ryker points his finger just inches from the guys face.

"Okay, rocker boy. Now get your fucking finger out of my face. Hey, sweetheart. The offer is always open. Bring red along with you. I'm always open for a challenge." The dark haired guy winks, nods toward Ivy, and then pushes his chair back and stands. His friends do the same. They walk away from the table leaving me standing there with the three people I've been avoiding all night.

"Jack, you're such a fucking liar. I thought you said you weren't fucking her anymore. You just can't keep it in your pants, can you?" Ivy bellows.

I'm not listening to this shit anymore. And obviously, neither is Ryker. He looks at me with emotionless eyes before he spins around and makes his way back to his table. I grip the serving tray a little tighter as I move around the two of them, trying desperately to escape this conversation. Because I don't like where it's heading.

"You know you're nothing to him. Nothing. A replacement. Did he tell you about her? The only reason he's fucking you is because you remind him of her."

"What the hell is wrong with you? I've always known you to be a bitch, but this is taking it too far," Annie says as she approaches.

I stop and look over my shoulder. Annie is standing in Ivy's face. I look to her right and see him. Jack. Wide stance, arms crossed, and eyes down. Defeated. I want to hug him. Tell him it's okay, but I can't. Because I don't know if it's okay. I have no idea what or who this crazy bitch is talking about.

"I'm not the one you need to be concerned about. It's him. He's the one still living in the past." Ivy points toward Jack.

"Jealousy looks like shit on you, Ivy. You need to rein it in before somebody else does it for you," Jack says as he looks at Ivy. His eyes are dark, sad, and glassy. Then he takes a step closer toward her.

The paleness of her green eyes brightens. Almost like a light flashes on in her mind. She's enjoying every second of this.

"Jealousy." She laughs. "We've already had this conversation, Jack. And you know... I don't do jealousy." She laughs louder.

"Why don't you tell Jovie about the last blue-eyed girl you thought you couldn't live without. Where is she now? Oh, I forgot she's not here because...?"

She stops mid-sentence looks over at me, and then back at Jack. She raises her right eyebrow, smirks, and then spins around and walks toward the bar.

That's it? She left without the punch line. As much dislike as I have for Ivy, which is more than I've ever felt for anyone else…ever. Still—I want to know. Who do I remind him of? More importantly—where is this mystery girl now?

"I'm fine. I just need to get out of here," Jack murmurs to Annie. She steps aside so he can walk around her. Within seconds, he's moving toward the door.

Even though he let me walk out of his life a few weeks ago, I can't let him leave here tonight. Not like this. Alone and hurt.

"Give me your tray and go." The sound of Naomi's voice pulls me from my thoughts.

"Are you sure?"

"Positive. Your shift ends in a few minutes anyway. He doesn't realize it yet, but he needs you." She forces a smile as she motions toward the door.

"Thanks," I mumble.

She grabs the tray as I drop it from my hands. Without looking back, I shuffle through the crowd until I reach the door. I push it open charging into the darkness in hopes of finding my heart.

I round the corner that faces the parking lot, but no Jack. So I travel toward the back of the building when a strong hand grips my waist. He pulls me into his body and buries his face into my neck. I know that smell. Clean. How does he always smell like he's just had a shower? Even after being in a cigarette smoke infested bar, he still smells like himself. So very Jack. I don't say anything. I let him hold me in silence because this is what he needs. What we both need. I wrap my arms around his neck as he lifts his head looking into my eyes. His glassy brown eyes tug at my soul.

"I'm sorry," he whispers.

His lips gently touch mine. Soft and slowly, he moves them from my lips nipping down my neck. His breathing is slow as he slides his hands down my sides and rests them on my waist.

"I'm sorry I let you walk out of my studio that night. I'm sorry I never called or texted you. I'm sorry for all the things Ivy said tonight. And on Thanksgiving. God, Jovie, I'm just so fucking sorry. I know you're not her. You could never be anybody's replacement."

"I shouldn't have walked out. All your rules. And then Ivy. I don't know what you want from me."

"I only want you. No rules. No past. Just you," he whispers.

"I want that, too." I nod slightly. His lips curl up into my favorite lop-sided grin before he wraps his hand around my wrist and leads us to the parking lot.

CHAPTER 24

SEVEN YEARS EARLIER

JACK

"WE'RE GOING TO that stupid Kappa Sig party first, and then I'm not sure after that. I really would rather just hang out here with you tonight. You know and watch you do your thing," Piper says as she leans on the counter.

"My thing?"

"The tattoos. It turns me on watching you put ink on some guy's body. Something about the way your hands move over his skin. One holding the ink thingy and the other one holding his skin tightly. I mean, honestly, I'm kinda getting hot thinking about it. What time is your next client?"

She slides around the counter until her body is touching mine. I swear her thoughts are completely warped. This is my passion. It's the love of art. And she just turned it into a joke. The thought of fucking her right now is the last thing on my mind. I have plans and they don't include her.

"In an hour, but sorry, it's a chick. So there won't be any guys here tonight to get your panties wet, so looks like you're out of luck."

"I didn't mean it like that. You're the only guy who gets my panties wet. Come here."

She skims her hand over the front of my jeans, stopping on my leg. Her lips find my neck and her hand moves to my dick.

Gentle massaging alternating with tugging is messing with my mind. Yes, I'm weak and easy. I want to take her to my station and fuck her against the wall. But not tonight. I'm not veering from the task at hand. She has clouded my vision for far too long with her hands, her mouth, and her pussy. No more until I know the truth.

"Not now, Piper. I'm the only one here. I can't chance somebody walking in."

Her breathing is heavier on my neck while her hands search for the entry to my pants. Fuck. She pops the button open as she lowers herself to the floor. She's on her knees, both hands in my pants.

"Stop. I said not now." I grab her wrists before her hands make it to my now throbbing dick. I shouldn't have let it get this far. She jumps up to her feet before tilting her head back so she can look into my eyes.

"What the hell, Jack?"

"I told you not right now."

"Fine. I gotta go anyway."

"Look, Piper. Don't be upset."

The chime goes off as the front door opens. A chick with long brown hair makes her way to the counter. I quickly button my pants. Piper grabs her phone and keys off the counter. She stands on her toes and kisses me on the cheek.

"I'll be over a little after midnight. Wait up for me." She rubs her hand over my dick and gives it a hard squeeze. Then she strolls out the front door leaving me to do my thing.

An hour later, I emerge from my station with a happy client. A simple cross on her right wrist. Even though it may seem like no big deal to me, but to her, it has meaning. Because if not, she wouldn't have found the courage to have it done. I give her the aftercare packet and collect the money. And she's out the door.

I grab my sketchbook from the drawer and flip through the pages. I've had this book forever. Old and new drawings combined make it more interesting. This particular book has character. It's only faces, nothing else. People I see on the street, at the bar, at restaurants. But it's also people I know… Annie, Fish, Piper, the chick who delivers pizza. Which I find odd. How many girls deliver pizza anyway?

"I'm here now if you need to leave," Annie shouts from down the hall as she stumbles through the side door.

I look at my phone. It's ten, so Piper and Maddie should be there by now. My chest is tight and my gut is full of dread. But this has to be done. I have to hunt down the truth.

"Are you sure you're okay to go alone?" Annie asks.

"Yes, I'm not a child. Well, not anymore. Plus I've been to many parties at that house. And don't forget that's where the asshole lives."

"I know, but still. I just hope I'm wrong and he's not even there. And you get your happily ever after—traveling the country with Piper."

"There's just one more thing before I go,"

"What?"

"Why in the hell did you sleep with him?"

"I drank too much. Then accidently fell into his bed. No biggie. I honestly don't even remember the sex. So that doesn't say much for him. But I'd rather not talk about my mistakes. You need to go. Find the truth. And text me when you get home. I have to know what goes down."

Annie squeezes my arm gently. Reassurance. That's exactly what I need.

"Thanks for covering for me," I holler as I make my way out the side door.

CHAPTER 25

JACK

MY HANDS ARE trembling as I slowly lower the handle to open the door to Kappa Sig's biggest party of the semester. I stumble over the threshold and maneuver my way through the crowd of drunks in search of Piper's long blonde hair. Unfortunately, I think every girl here may be blonde. And then I see her. Maddie Foster. Piper's best friend and a complete fucking bitch. I move toward her until I'm close enough to grab her wrist. She spins around—takes one look at my face and her smile immediately fades.

"Where is she, Maddie?"

"Where is who, Jack?" She smirks.

I squeeze my eyes shut and silently count to ten. I do this to keep from knocking that smart-ass look off her face. I know she's a chick, and I would never hit her, but she's made it her mission over the last year to piss me off every chance she gets.

"So are you meditating now… in hopes of envisioning her exact location?" She laughs.

I clench my teeth as I pull her in closer. "I'm not in the mood to play games with you tonight. Tell me where Piper is."

"What makes you think I know? I am not her keeper." She rolls her eyes and pulls her wrist from my grip.

"I know she's here. So take your damn phone out and send her a warning. Let her know the bullshit ends tonight!"

"Wow, Jack. I didn't know you had it in you to be so

possessive. I have to say I'm more than impressed. Maybe even a little turned on." She winks and then leans over toward the girl standing next to her. They both laugh. She takes a couple of steps toward the crowd, and I watch her hand move toward her back pocket. She pulls out her phone, and then I know. I know Piper is here with *him.*

She's quickly lost in the crowd, so I return my focus on finding my girlfriend. Looking over my shoulder, I notice the staircase I've been avoiding since walking through the front door—because up those stairs is the last place I want to find her. I drag my hand through my hair and take a deep breath. I put one foot in front of the other as I make myself trudge up each step. When I reach the top, I turn slightly to see Maddie standing at the bottom peering up at me. Her eyes are dark and she's moving her head from side to side. Ignoring her plea, my eyes return to the empty hallway in front of me. Shuffling slowly, I stop in front of each door. Leaning in, I bring my ear close to listen for voices. One room, two rooms, three rooms and nothing. My heart rate increases with each stop I make. When I reach the last door on the right, I hear a voice. *Her voice. Piper.*

Even though I knew what I might find tonight, I'm still not prepared to hear her moaning behind the closed door. I take a deep breath before placing my hand on the knob. Turning it slightly to the right, I push open the door. My body freezes as heat rises to my face. The image in front of me will be forever imprinted in my mind. Piper's naked body is straddling some guy, and she's rocking her hips back and forth. Her body quivers just before she throws her head back and screams his name.

"Caleb!"

Mother. Fucking. Caleb. And I lose it.

She rolls off him, neither realizing I'm standing here watching my life crumble before my eyes.

"I'll see you Thursday—" Piper says to Caleb as she turns around to get her clothes. She sees me standing in front of the open door and stops.

"Fuck, you scared me!" she screams.

"Is that all you have to say? I walk in on you fucking that piece of shit and all you can say is I scared you?"

"No, I mean. Shit. How long have you been standing there?"

"Again, Piper. What the fuck is wrong with you? Does it matter how long I've been standing here? If it makes you feel any better, I'll be glad to tell you that I saw you straddling his dick long enough to get off. There. Does that make you feel better?"

"No! No! No! This is not happening. Jack, you are not here. You can't be. Please!" she screams.

"Please what? Forget I just saw the two of you fucking. My girlfriend and my former friend. It ain't happening." I gather her clothes off the floor and throw them at her.

"Thanks for letting me waste a year of my life on you. And I'm not even gonna ask how long it's been going on. Because it doesn't fucking matter. I'm done with your whoring ass, and you!" I point toward Caleb, who is now dressed and sitting on the edge of the bed.

"Man, you're a piece of work. You deserve each other. I hope you have a happy life together because I'm done. With both of you." I have to take a couple of steps backward toward the hall because, if not, I am going to completely lose it.

"Call me what you want, Jack, but you're the one who couldn't keep her satisfied. If you would've, then she wouldn't be fucking me. So, obviously, you need to step up your game before you take on another chick." Caleb laughs.

"Or maybe she's just a whore who can't be happy with one dick or maybe not even two. For all I know, she's fucking you, me, and ten other guys. So, now would be the time for you to shut the fuck up."

"I agree, she's a whore, but so is your beloved Annie. Remember I fucked her, too. Your girlfriend and your best friend. Fucking classic."

In five steps, I'm standing in front of Caleb, who is still sitting on the bed.

"What's wrong? Can't handle the truth? That every chick you care anything about has crawled into my bed for the best fuck of their life." He stands. Smirking, he looks over my shoulder at Piper quickly dressing. She collects all of her things and hurries to the door.

"We still on for Thursday night?" He tilts his head back and lets out a chuckle. When his head returns to center, I'm ready. Fist clenched, I draw my right arm back and then release it forward with everything I've got. My fist connects with his jaw, and the impact vibrates back up my arm and stops on my shoulder. He falls back on the bed without hesitation.

"You son-of-a-bitch," he mutters as he spits a small amount of blood into his hand.

He doesn't jump up swinging or even mutter another word.

Before I'm completely out of his bedroom, I turn and say, "By the way, that hit you just took was for what you said about Annie."

I jog down the stairs with my phone in hand. My mind is racing a million miles a minute. Piper just walked out without a fight. Not her usual personality, but it makes it easier on me. This entire night has turned out much differently than I thought it would. I'm not mad or even hurt. And I think it's mostly because I knew what I would probably find. I've suspected it for weeks. It still hurts, but nothing like the initial shock of Annie's confession. I shoot Annie a text to let her know I'm leaving and will call her when I get to my apartment. Next, I avoid anybody and everybody I know as I search for the front door.

When I make it to my truck, I remember that I forgot to lock my doors. This is only evident because I see Piper sitting in the passenger seat chewing her fingernails. I fucking knew everything had gone entirely too smoothly. I grab the handle of the passenger side door and pull on it. Locked. Fucking bitch.

"Open the door and get the fuck out," I holler with my face inches from the window.

She shakes her head. Indicating that she has no intentions of getting out.

I pound my fist on the window hard, but not hard enough to shatter glass. She cups her hands and rests her face in them. If she's crying, I really don't give a shit. She should have thought about what would happen when I found out before she spread her legs for that asshole. I walk around to my door and open it. I slide in behind the steering wheel.

"Get out of my truck, Piper. I'm going home."

"Take me with you. Please," she begs.

"No, I'm done with this night and with you." She's not budging. Fuck.

"I only want to talk. Just hear me out. Please, Jack. Don't throw us away."

"You took care of that when you decided to fuck Caleb. There's nothing to talk about. So you can either get out on your own, or I'm gonna pull you out." She knows better than that. I will never put my hands on her. I guess I'm stuck. Either sit here all night listening to her bullshit, call somebody to come get me, or drive her to her apartment and maybe her roommate can get her out.

"Fine. I'll take you home, but I'm not coming in. Our relationship is over. No discussion."

She doesn't utter another word. At least not until we're on the road heading back toward her apartment.

"Take me to your place. I don't want to go home. I need to be with you. I need you to hold me and tell me everything is gonna be okay."

"Everything isn't okay. What part of you fucking Caleb ended our relationship do you not understand? Damn."

It's late and traffic isn't too bad. Hopefully, I'll have her home and out of my life in less than ten minutes. My mind is drifting in and out of thoughts about how fucked up this entire situation really is, so I'm not paying attention when she grabs my wrist and pulls my right hand from the steering wheel. I twist and pull my hand trying like hell to free it, but it's too hard to fight her and pay attention to the road.

"Piper, let go of me. I'm driving."

She attempts to crawl into my lap, but I'm able to push her back with the hand she's holding.

"I'm not giving up, Jack. We can fix us. We have plans. Remember? We are leaving at the end of the semester. You have to help me get us through this."

I decide that it might be better just to agree with her than to fight her. Because, at this point, she's just seconds from straddling me while I'm driving down the road.

"Okay. Once we get to your place, we'll talk. But I'm not making any promises. Is that good enough?" I ask.

"Perfect. I knew you'd come around." She releases my hand so I'm able to secure the steering wheel again.

I think she may be losing her mind. I don't think she's drunk because I don't smell any alcohol. Maybe she's in shock. Fuck if I know. I glance over at her, and she's back in her seat with her seatbelt secured. I let out a sigh of relief as I bring my eyes back into focus on the road.

"Jack, watch out—that car—it's in our lane—"

CHAPTER 26

JACK

DRUNK DRIVER. THAT'S who hit us head on. I woke up two days later in the hospital with a broken nose, broken wrist, and a concussion. Piper. Well, she didn't wake up. She left me to grieve alone. The fact is, she should have never been in the truck with me that night. If I would've called Annie to come get me and left her at the party with Maddie and Caleb. But I didn't, so her death is on me. And for that, my life is forever changed.

The banging on the front door finally stops. Only for a minute or maybe two. Now it's at my window.

"Go away." I roll over and pull my pillow over my head.

"If you don't open your door, I'm gonna break this motherfucking window," Fish's deep voice rumbles.

"Fine. Break the damn window. I don't give two shits."

So, he did. With a tire iron. And then his big ass crawls in avoiding being cut to shreds.

"Now, I did what you told me to. I broke your window. So you need to get your ass out of bed, take a shower, and come to work."

"Umm… no. How many times do I have to tell you, Annie, and Stone my fucking wrist is broken, so I can't work."

"Your left wrist is broken and you are right handed. You can do something. Even if you don't actually perform the task of creating any tattoos, you'll be there. Out of this apartment. You can sketch, collect money. Shit, there's plenty you can do. But what you're not gonna do is stay locked up in this apartment forever. And what about school?"

"What about it. I'm not going back. I'm done."

"You're not done. Get your ass up now," he says as he rolls me off the bed.

"Fine, I'll go to work, but school is out of the question."

I pull a t-shirt over my head and look around for jeans and boots.

"Wait a second. Carry your nasty ass to the shower. You haven't been out of this apartment for over a week, so something tells me that it's been at least that long since you showered."

He's right. I haven't done much of anything but lay around in bed—on the couch—on the floor. Just wherever my ass lands is where I sleep.

* * * * *

I stagger into Southern Stain behind Fish. It's quiet, which means everybody's busy. I make it to my station and unlock the door. Annie is waiting for me on the other side. Not surprising.

"Before you say a word, I'm not discussing my life with you today. The only reason I'm here is because Fish would have picked me up out of bed and brought me against my will. So I saved him the trouble and came on my own." I deadpan.

"It's not your fault. The guy responsible is in jail. Nobody got him out. And Caleb's gone. Came in, got all his shit, and left. Looked like hell, by the way. I went to the funeral alone. I felt like I owed it to her and of course, to you. Your parents left right after you woke up. Your dad wants me to be sure you get back to school ASAP. Did I forget anything? Hmm… Oh, and stop blaming yourself. I know that's why you've been on lockdown in your apartment."

"Are you done?"

"Yes, unless you want to talk about what exactly happened

that night?"

"No. I'm not discussing what happened the night I found her with Caleb. The only thing I will say is that I should have made her get out of my truck. If I would've, she'd still be alive. But I didn't, so she's gone. So, yes, it's my fault. And I will never forgive myself for it. I failed at taking care of her. And that's all she ever wanted from me.

"She was sleeping with another guy, too, Jack. I know this hurts, but she wasn't yours to protect."

"Yes, she was. Even after all the lies and fucking around, I still loved her. That night, I was so angry I pretended like she never mattered, but she did. Hell, I was ready to give up my life to follow her across the country. So, just because she was fucking Caleb doesn't shut my feelings off. It actually makes everything worse."

"Worse? How?"

"To know that I loved her so much, and she didn't love me back. There's no way she could have loved me like I loved her. Because I would have never fucked another chick. She was it for me." My eyes are burning, itching. I'm a grown man—one who cried like a baby that day in the hospital when I found out that Piper was gone. But, since then, I've been able to refrain from letting the tears fall. And today will not be any different.

"Maybe you need to talk to somebody. You know, like a counselor. Someone to help you deal with the feelings your having," Annie says as she walks over to me.

"Fuck no. I'll be fine. Just let me grieve, alone. Please." She wraps her arms around my waist and rests her face against my chest.

"I love you, Jack. And we're gonna get through this. Just promise me you won't let this change you. You're a kind soul, and I don't want you to ever lose that."

I bend over slightly and kiss the top of her head. I want to tell her that I'm already changed. My life has no purpose now.

But I don't want her to worry, so I just agree with her, and hopefully, she will let me be. At least, for a while. "I'll always be Jack. That will never change. I just don't know how long it'll be before I am able to find my way back to this life." She releases her hold and looks up into my eyes. Smiling, she walks toward the door.

"I'm just one door down if you need me. Just promise you'll stay most of the day. Then maybe we can grab dinner. Just you and me."

"Sounds great. Pull the door too, on your way out." She nods and closes my door. Leaving me alone. And alone is exactly where I want to be.

CHAPTER 27

JOVIE

THE VIBRATION OF the tattoo machine sends chills down the left side of my body and around my waist. There's no pain, only a sensation of wanting more. But with the small starter tattoo Jack is creating along my rib cage, more will be a definite possibility. It's Valentine's Day and Annie's birthday, so we have double celebrating to do.

"This is the same tattoo that you were gonna get the first day you showed up here. You know, the day you got the piercing?" Jack asks as he makes fluid strokes spreading the ink along the skin over my ribs.

"Yeah, I already told you that. Did you forget?"

"No. I was just wondering if you had that piece of paper with the sketch of the 'just breathe' encased in an infinity sign when you came in the shop that day," he mumbles.

"Yes, remember? I had it out but put it back in my purse when I changed my mind."

"Yeah, you're right. I do remember, but where did you tell me you got the sketch?"

"I found it in a box under my sister's bed. She didn't... have a tattoo, but this is the one she always wanted. At least, I think it was."

I have spent every night in Jack's bed since the bar fiasco.

147

Every night all night. He's thrown away all of those stupid rules for me. I'm the one person who makes him feel real again. At least, that's what he says. For me, placing my ear on his chest above his heart gives me the rhythm I need to cover me with the peace that has freed me from my anxiety. I didn't go home for Christmas or New Years. Spending the holidays with him was difficult. He shuts down during certain times. And those holidays were the worst. He's never told me his entire story, and I don't pry because he will. When he's ready. I know something bad happened to him several years ago that involved a girlfriend. And he's never picked up the pieces and moved on until me.

"Did she have anxiety, too?" he asks.

"Not really sure. I was so much younger than she was, so we didn't talk about those kinds of problems. We mostly talked about my friends, her college classes, and how she loved her life." My eyes fill with moisture, but I don't understand why. We talk about her some, but I don't usually feel like crying. Maybe it's because I'm getting this tattoo. Her tattoo.

"This tattoo is perfect for you. And it looks beautiful," he says as he leans in closer to finish his task.

"Do you care if I hang on to the sketch? I want to show Annie."

"Sure. I don't need it anymore. I have the real thing."

He sprays the antiseptic onto the tattoo, and the coolness feels amazing against my hot skin. Jack folds the sketch into a small square and shoves it into his pocket. Then he helps me up off the chair and grabs the mirror.

"Wow. Jack. It's beautiful. More beautiful than I would have imagined. You are so talented," I mumble as I twist my body slightly to get a better view.

Getting this tattoo is a sign. It's my okay to go back to the gravesite. My life is better—since I found Jack. My anxiety is nonexistent. I'm only seeing Dr. Birch twice a month. School is great. And I'm happy. This is the life I've been missing. This is the life I'm meant to have. And it feels unbelievable.

"You're beautiful. Thank you for not giving up on me. And for loving me in spite of, well, you know, my multitude of problems."

"We all have problems. Look at me. I'm a living, breathing, walking, talking, bundle of issues."

"Yeah, but you're mine. And that's all that matters." He takes the mirror from my hand and lays it on the counter.

His hands drift from my bare stomach up to my bra. Greedy lips follow behind. He carefully unhooks my bra and it falls to the floor. He gently walks me backward until I'm pressed against the wall. Warm lips find my nipple. Slow, gentle tugs followed by painful nibbles are the perfect combination. He alternates between my right and then my left before moving up my chest to my collarbone. His warm tongue moves from my shoulder to my neck. The moisture growing between my legs quickly turns to a drenching wetness with a throbbing that needs his attention— now. As if he could sense my desire, he slides his hand down my stomach and into my leggings.

"No panties?" his breath warm on my neck.

"Hmm… is that a problem?" I whisper.

"Not. At. All."

He slides his fingers through the wetness as I squeeze my legs together and press my hips into the movement of his touch.

"I need more," I whisper into his lips.

My tongue darts out, quickly licking his lips, and then moves along his jaw line to his neck.

"Tell me what you want, Jovie."

"For you to take my leggings off, put your dick inside of me, and make me scream," I say between kisses and nips on his neck. My heart is hammering against my chest wall. I'm losing control of the grinding of my hips. Faster. Harder. Faster. Harder. I grab his hand with mine and press it into my center. Then my fingers and hips move in unison with his. Deep breaths in and out, and holy fucking shit, it hits me like a load of bricks. The tingling sensation starts at my toes, travels up my legs to the pit of my stomach.

"Jack. Oh, God," I bellow, not caring who is listening outside the door.

I ride out this feeling for what seems like minutes or hours, and then I'm spent. His hand slides out of my pants, hooking his fingers on the waistband and pulling them down past my ass and my knees. I manage to step out of them and kick them to the side. Then I drop to my knees. I bite his inner thighs softly alternating right and then left. He's still clothed, but I like to tease him, and I'm not in any hurry to rip his pants off—yet.

My mouth moves up his leg to his crotch. God, that smell. It's all Jack, and it freaking turns me on just about as much as anything he can do with his mouth or fingers.

I inhale deeply as I place my mouth over his covered dick. My warm breath is toying with his need. I can feel it. I feel it in the heaviness of his erection and tightness of his inner thigh. I nip, bite, and rub until he's on his knees in front of me. His mouth crashes against mine as he pulls my naked body onto his lap. He moves his hips causing friction against my already sensitive spot. I don't know how much stimulation I can take. Those jeans have to come off. Now. I wiggle a couple more seconds and then lean in closer.

"Your pants, take them off."

Unbuttoning them, I push the waist down and he lifts his ass off the floor. I lift my right leg moving off him while he shimmies out of his jeans and boxers. Then I return my leg so I'm straddling him once again. My fingers fidget with his shirt before he yanks it off over his head. He throws it across the room and then focuses his attention back on me. His hands caress my body—sliding up my stomach, arms, breasts, shoulders, neck, and when he reaches my face, he holds onto each cheek. He tilts his forehead until it's resting on mine.

"You're so fucking beautiful." The whisper of his voice drives me crazy.

I close my eyes and move my lips to his. The kiss is slow, wet, and a bit sloppy, but it's fucking what I need as I slide my wetness over the length of his dick. Back and forth. Up and down. The tip slides in and then back out. He does it again and again. He's teasing me.

"Jack, stop playing with me and give me what I want."

He wraps his hands around my waist, lifts me up quickly, and then slams me down onto all of his hardness. This doesn't give me time to adjust to his width, so I scream and then take in a breath, and then cry out again. He immediately places his hand over my mouth.

"Shh! I don't want Fish or Stone coming in here. And they will come with all the screaming. Are you okay? Did I hurt you?" He's stopped moving. I'm sitting here with all that is hard, stretching me, preparing me for what is yet to come.

"No, it just felt so good. Sorry. I forgot where we were."

He slides the tips of his fingers up my back. The light touch of his fingertips sends a chill down my spine. I grind my hips into him, and he meets me with thrust after thrust.

"Open your eyes, Jovie. I need to see you. To know it's you here with me. Feeling every single movement with me." He moans.

I give him what he wants—forcing my eyelids open, I'm greeted with his brown eyes staring, watching, wanting.

"This is forever," he says before he throws his head back, closes his eyes, and rides his orgasm to the end.

I wrap my legs tighter around his waist and shift forward, placing all of my weight on him. I rotate my hips as I press forward. He moves his hand up my leg and to my center, but I'm there. I scream again, but the tingling running all through my body is so intense, this scream won't stop until the end.

When I'm back from the most amazing feeling in the world,

my eyes find his—again. He greets me with his sexy as hell grin.

"Sorry for that last scream." I giggle.

"We're gonna have to stop doing this in public places, woman. I never think of you as a screamer at home, but damn. Get you in a building with people shuffling up and down the hall and you scream so loud, they can hear you two buildings over." He winks and smiles.

I know he's kidding, but I can't help myself. The sex is freaking great.

"It's your fault,"

"How is it my fault you scream every time I put my dick inside you?"

"Because you're the best. You cause me to lose all self-control, so I scream. It actually makes my orgasm last longer."

"Screaming makes your orgasm last longer?"

"Yes. Can't explain it but it does."

He lifts me off him. We trek across the room to the restroom. He cleans both of us up with a warm washcloth and then we dress. I know he has more clients today, but I'm feeling needy.

"How late do you have to work tonight?" I ask.

"Until about seven. You know it's Annie's birthday party tonight."

"Yeah, I forgot, but I can go. I'm off." I smile as he leans down and places a soft kiss on my cheek.

He wraps his big arms around me, squeezing so tight, I can hardly breathe. I'm about to scream—again—when he releases me and looks into my eyes.

"You know you didn't ask about the pill this time. Did you forget?" I ask.

He always asks me if I'm on the pill before we have sex. At first, no condom, no sex. But now, since we have an agreement that we are together—only us. Then he's okay with the pill.

"No, I trust you. And believe me when I tell you, you are

one of only about a handful of people I trust. If you weren't on the pill, you would say. So I've stopped worrying about it."

"Thank you for trusting me." I slide my hands up his chest and back down. I wrap my arms around his waist pulling his body into mine.

"I wish we could stand here like this for the rest of the day, but my clients are going to start rolling in," he utters.

I place a kiss on his chest before he walks with me out of his workstation and to the lobby.

"I'll see you tonight." I smile.

"Can you be dressed and at my place by seven?"

"I can do anything for you."

He leans down and kisses me on the lips.

"Text me later," he says.

I'm smiling because he makes me so freaking happy. I open the door, walk into the parking lot, and head for my car.

CHAPTER 28

JACK

"CHAMPAGNE." I GIVE the bubbling liquid to Jovie and she accepts with a smile.

"Mr. Alexander, are you contributing to the delinquency of a minor?" She laughs.

Personally, I don't find it amusing, but I'll let her have her fun.

"Very funny, Ms. Blake. Hilarious. You'll be twenty in a few weeks, anyway."

"Twenty is still not old enough to drink in this state. Even though I can sell it, I'm not supposed to consume it. But tonight is a special occasion. So I'll drink as much as you want to bring me."

"You're not worried I'm trying to get you drunk so I can take advantage of you?"

"Why would I worry about that when you can take advantage of me sober? You taking advantage of me is my favorite past time." She takes a sip of her drink. She looks at me over her glass. Those incredible blue eyes that scared me away at first now allow me to see inside her soul. And it's beautiful just like her outer appearance. With her help, I have been able to pick up the pieces of my broken life and put it back together.

"Are you still going with me to my sister's gravesite tomorrow?

She steps in closer before resting her hand on my chest.

"Yes. But I want you to be absolutely sure that you are ready to go."

"I'm ready. Dr. Birch says it's time. I need the closure. I need to be able to go without having a nervous breakdown. Well, not a real breakdown. I'm better now. My life is good. I have you."

"You'll always have me. I'm not going anywhere. At least not without you." I laugh.

She told me the story about her sister dying. Well, not really the story. A few weeks ago, she explained that she had an older sister who died several years ago. That is the source of her anxiety. She's buried somewhere in town. And tomorrow she wants to introduce me to her. Sounds creepy, but Jovie is my light. She pulled me out of a place I never want to go again. So I will do anything for her. Anything.

"Jack, can you come here for a minute? Fish needs you out front." I look over my shoulder and it's Stone. His blue eyes are wild, continually scanning the room. Something is up.

"Sure." I reach for Jovie's hand.

"No, just you. Naomi will stay here with her. It's a guy problem." I give my glass to Jovie and force a smile. She shrugs her shoulders and takes my champagne.

I follow Stone to the front of the house. As we approach the window, he stops and turns to look at me.

"I don't know what the hell is going on. But this shit is not going down at my house. Got it?"

"What are you talking about? You came and got me, brought me up to the front door, and now you're giving me vague random speeches about some shit I know nothing about." I grab the front door handle just as Stone slams his hand against the door, preventing me from opening it.

"What the hell, man? Fucking tell me. What's going on?"

"Fish, Ryker, and a couple other guys are out there with Caleb."

"What the fuck is he doing here?"

"Did you know he is back in town?"

"Yeah, Fish told me back in November. He said that he's working at The Hard Ink."

I pull on the doorknob again, but Stone's not budging.

"You brought me up here and told me that son-of-a-bitch is in the yard, but you won't let me go take care of it?"

"There's something else that you need to know."

"What? I wish you motherfuckers would stop with all this 'I know but you don't' bullshit. What else do I need to know?"

"He showed up about twenty minutes ago. He's shitfaced. I mean can barely walk."

"Is he driving?" I ask. Like I fucking care.

"No, he's with some brown haired chick. She must be driving. But anyway, he's trying to get in to see Jovie. He is asking about her. Says he needs to see her. To talk to her."

"What the fuck? Let me out the front door before I kick it in. Seriously, Stone. Open the door."

He removes his hand from the door. And I yank it open. Charging into the front yard, I notice Fish is holding him around his chest escorting him back to his vehicle. Some chick with long brown hair is sitting in the driver's seat. Fish pulls open the passenger door, shoves him inside, and then slams it shut. I sprint to the end of the driveway, but it's a no-go because Fish grabs my arm to stop me. Caleb's window is down, and as soon as our eyes meet, the car stops.

"Does she fucking know?" he slurs from inside the car.

I break away from Fish and jog down the sidewalk until I'm standing in front of his window. He's drunk. So damn drunk.

"Stay the fuck away from her. I don't know what's going on. But if you go near Jovie, I swear it will be the last thing your useless ass does."

"She doesn't know, does she? But she will. You can count on it, brother. You can fucking count on it." He stares at me until the car is out of sight. I turn around and move back toward the house.

Fish places his hand on my shoulder, bringing me to a stop. "What?"

"Nothing, man. I'm wondering what he's talking about."

"No clue. But you don't think… I can't even bring myself to say it." I look away.

"No, I don't think he's fucking Jovie. If that's what you're thinking. He's been gone for years. Why he'd show up and start hooking up with your girl doesn't make sense. There's more to it. Maybe I'll head over to The Hard Ink tomorrow and get some answers from him."

"No. Leave him alone. I'll take care of him if he harasses Jovie. Otherwise, just let him be. Let him fucking be." I look at Fish and he nods.

"I'm heading back inside to get Jovie. I gotta get out of here. Too much shit for one night," I say.

"Okay, man. See ya." He walks toward the house.

This means nothing. Everything is perfect with Jovie and me. She's mine. I know she would never hook up with some piece of shit like Caleb. I run my hand through my hair as I turn and head toward the house. I'm going to get my girl and get the hell out of this place.

CHAPTER 29

JOVIE

"ARE YOU FUCKING anybody else?" Jack asks with ease. Like he believes it's true, or maybe he's sleeping with somebody else and this is his way of telling me. We've been in this relationship about three months. What if he can't handle it and wants out.

"No. Why would you even ask that?"

He walks over to the bed, sits down beside me, and looks into my eyes.

"No reason, just making sure." He smiles as he wraps his arms around my waist pulling me into his lap. I straddle his warm, almost naked body. This guy makes me feel things I've never felt. To have been such an asshole in the beginning, he has recovered nicely.

He closes his eyes as my hands massage his neck and scalp. Then I can't help myself. I have to ask.

"Are you fucking anybody else?"

"You're kidding me, right?" His eyes snap open. Dark eyes stare back at me.

"No. You asked me, so why can't I ask you?"

"Those are the most ridiculous words I've ever heard come off those red lips." He gently moves his finger around my mouth. Then over my lips. My tongue darts out and licks my bottom lip. Slowly. He slips his finger into my mouth. I wrap my lips around it as I tilt my head back and close my eyes. I lick, suck, and slowly release his finger. He drags his wet finger down my chin, neck, and chest. The lifting of my tank top prompts me to raise my arms above my head. Off with the tank leaves me bare, naked, and still straddling this beautiful guy.

He rolls me over until I'm on my back. He's hovering over me—so close, the warmth of his skin is all I feel. He lowers himself with ease until his lips are on my breast. Licking and sucking, one and then the other. Moving his mouth down my stomach nipping my skin until he reaches my panties. The panties go sailing across the room in less than three seconds. Warm breath on my inner thighs as he alternates between kissing, blowing, and nipping. I spread my legs in desperation. He needs to give me something. His tongue, a finger, his dick. I lift my hips off the bed trying to make contact with something on his body. He suddenly pulls his head back.

"Jack. Stop," I plead.

"You want me to stop, babe?"

"No, not stop, but no more teasing."

He laughs. Then he presses his lips to my center. The spot that controls all my feeling and emotion during sex. He licks, flicks, and then sucks. Over and over and over until my legs wrap around his neck and my ass lifts off the bed. He slides his hands under my bottom to keep me exactly where he wants.

"Holy fucking shit," I yell.

My hips buck against his face. The suction is almost more than my sensitive little spot can take. I swear my eyes roll back in my head as my entire body trembles from the waist down. Deep breathing in and out is all I can do. It's as if I just ran a damn marathon. My legs are weak and my senses are on high alert. He lifts his head and crawls up my body. When he reaches my neck, he blows his warm breath along my skin until he reaches my ear.

"I love it when you say words like fucking and shit when I make you come. It is such a turn on."

"Take your boxers off," I whisper.

The words are barely out of my mouth before his bare skin

presses against mine. He pushes his hardness into my center as he shifts above me. He rocks his hips from side to side, and then moves down slightly until his tip is inside of me. I wrap my legs around his ass and push. He holds back for a second before advancing the tip in a bit farther and then pulling out. He continues this little ritual until he can't take it anymore. He plunges into me with force. Hard and fast, then he slows and finds a rhythm. He moves in and out… slow, smooth, and gentle. The friction—the pressure—is perfect. His chest rises and falls as his breathing speeds up.

"I love you, Jovie." He moans.

A tear rolls down my cheek. I have no idea where it came from, but there are more. I tuck my face into his chest as he lowers himself onto my body once he finds his release. I don't want him to see my tears. Who cries during sex?

He rolls off me. Grabbing my hand, he pulls it into his chest and places it over his heart.

"Do you feel that?" he asks.

"Of course, why?"

"Until I met you, there wasn't beating. Only existing. Thank you."

"I thought we weren't going to say thank you or you're welcome after sex anymore." I giggle.

"You don't understand that over the last few months, you have given me a life that I want to wake up to every morning."

"Jack, I love you." I turn to face him. He smiles and kisses me on the nose.

"I love you, too." He wraps his arms around me pulling me in tight.

"I want to keep you here. This close to me, forever."

"I want that, too." I nuzzle my face into his chest and let him hold me.

My eyelids are heavy even though I know that I need to shower before sleeping, but I'm here with him. He's holding me so tightly, I'm afraid he's gonna break me. But not on purpose. Because he loves me. Just as I'm drifting, he moves.

"I've gotta get cleaned up, and so do you. Come shower with me." He mumbles as he rolls out of bed.

"In a few minutes. I'm gonna lie here for a bit."

He walks across the bedroom naked and beautiful. I bet he has at least twenty tattoos, and I want to count every one. The bathroom door closes, and now I'm wide awake. So I sit up and swing my legs off the side of the bed. As I reach for my phone on the nightstand, my hand bumps an empty glass and it tumbles to the floor.

"Shit."

I bend over to retrieve it, saying silent thanks that it's empty. So no mess to clean up. I glance over toward the nightstand. There's an unfamiliar sketchbook on the bottom shelf. I bet this is one of the originals. I really want to see how much his art has progressed. He won't care. He loves me.

I pick up the glass and grab the sketchbook. Then I place the glass back in its spot on the nightstand before leaning back into the pillows getting comfortable. I flip through the first few pages. It's faces. Only faces. I recognize Annie, Fish, and even Stone. They look different. Younger. But there are lots of people I don't know. Which isn't surprising since this book is obviously several years old.

The shower goes off and Jack cracks the bathroom door.

"I thought you were gonna join me," he says.

"I know, but I'm looking at your art. Is that okay?"

"Yeah, sure." He pushes the door closed and I continue flipping pages.

About mid-way through the book, my eyes lock onto another set of blue eyes. Her eyes. My eyes. Blonde hair. Small nose. And the smile that is so big, you can see it before she walks into a room. She is happy, smiling, almost glowing. She's alive. In this sketch, she's alive.

The door to the bathroom opens, and in an instant, Jack is standing in front of me. I look up from the book. The tears are falling. Again. But this time, I know why I'm crying. I just don't know what to do about it. What to say.

"Jovie, you're crying. What's wrong?" He drops down in front of me. His brown eyes look at me and then down at the picture.

"Where did you find that book?"

I'm still speechless. I reach deep into my soul to find the words. Because the shit's about to get real. Real fucking ugly. My mind is reeling in self-doubt. Nothing makes sense anymore, but yet everything is here in my face.

"You didn't want me to find this book, did you?"

"No, I don't care that you found it. I just haven't seen it in a while."

I look down at the picture and then back at Jack.

"How did you know her?" I ask.

"Who? What are you talking about?"

"Her. How in the fuck did you know her?" I point to the picture in the book of the blonde girl with my same blue eyes.

"It's a long story. But I can assure you that everything she broke in a year's time, you've fixed in three months."

My breathing is fast and my chest is tight. The tingling in my face turns to numbness. I'm drowning. There's no way out. I drop the book, as I lay flat on the bed. As I close my eyes, I inhale deeply and then exhale. Inhale. Exhale. Inhale. Exhale. *Breathe and it will all be over with soon.*

"Jovie, are you okay?" I hear the fear in his voice. But I don't look at him. Not now.

He takes both of my hands in his, but I pull away.

"Don't fucking touch me," I pant.

He stands, runs his finger through his hair as he paces the entire room. Over and over again. Until I can breathe again. I'm exhausted, but I slowly pull myself up to a sitting position. Jack stops pacing. He looks at me and then at the book on the floor. His thoughts are racing. I can see it in his eyes.

"Tell me who the girl in the sketchbook is," I demand.

"Why? It doesn't matter. It was years ago. I swear there's nobody, but you."

"Fucking tell me, Jack!"

"Her name was Piper. She was my girlfriend when I was nineteen. Some really bad shit went down. And I don't know, Jovie. This is hard for me. I don't talk about her or what happened because it fucked me up for a long time. Well, until you."

I stand beside the bed. My legs are too shaky. They won't hold me up, so I drop to the floor.

"Tell me what happened to her."

"I walked in on her fucking a former friend of mine at a frat party. She climbed into my truck. She begged me not to leave her. I didn't know what to do, so I decided to take her home. Let her roommate help me get her out. But we never made it. A drunk driver hit us head on. It killed her instantly."

He drops his head as he sits down on the floor beside me. He flips through the book until he comes to her picture.

"It's her. She's the one with the blue eyes. She's the reason you asked me if I was an angel. Ivy was talking about her that night at the bar. It's always been about her. Am I right, Jack?"

"No, Jovie. It's never been about her. It's you. Always you."

He crawls over closer to me. I take the book from him and look at her one last time.

"You're wrong. My entire life has been about her. Her death has dictated every decision my parents made for me. And now you. How did this happen? You fucking found me. You knew this entire time. Didn't you?"

"What the hell are you talking about? You're not making any sense."

"Piper was my sister! You asshole. And you knew it. Didn't

you? Didn't you?"

My mind is hazy and I'm off balance. He knew the whole time. Or maybe he didn't know. It doesn't fucking matter.

I stand, clutching the sketchbook in my hand. I don't know what to do. How to act. I've never felt so much grief, so much anger, so much hurt, so much uncertainty. I look down at him.

"Jovie, I…" His eyes are vacant.

"Say something. Say fucking anything. Don't just sit there like that!"

Nothing. He says nothing.

I hurl the sketchbook across the room before grabbing my clothes and getting dressed. When I turn around Jack is standing directly in front of me. He grabs my arms and looks into my eyes.

"I didn't fucking know. I swear to you."

"Let go of me. This is too much. I have to go."

"Are you coming back?"

"Are you fucking kidding me?" I step back away from him. Grabbing my bag, I stuff my phone inside and grab my keys.

My wobbly legs carry me out of the room and out the front door. He doesn't come after me—again.

CHAPTER 30

JACK

I STAND IN the center of my bedroom. The same place I stood over a month ago, when Jovie introduced me to my worst fucking nightmare. I still don't know how the hell it happened. But now, since I've had some time to sort things out. It is becoming much clearer. I never met Piper's family. She was always very private. Hell, I really didn't know Piper. But we were young. And looking back, I know she was running from something. Most likely herself... her life. I was only a temporary fix in her addiction to finding something different. Something better.

And that tattoo. Jovie's tattoo. It is one that I designed for Piper over seven years ago. The sketch she gave me is mine. It is my drawing, only I never got around to putting any ink on Piper. The day that Jovie told me she had found it in a box in her dead sister's room, I should have figured it out. How else do I explain her having the sketch?

Finally, Caleb. He somehow must have found out about Jovie. That's the only way to explain why he showed up looking for her. Jovie is not Piper, and I know she wouldn't screw around with him. She's not that person. She loves me. I truly believe that.

"Are you ready?"

"Yeah," I grab my bag off the bed before walking out into the living room.

"You sure you want to do this? It's a long trip."

Annie's standing in the doorway with my keys in her hand.

"I'm sure. I have to talk to her. That night, I hardly said

165

anything. I was too shocked. But now that I've had some time to sort things out, I have to go."

She drops the keys in my hand and wraps her arms around me for a hug.

"Do you even know what you're gonna say?"

"No, but what I do know is that I miss her. And every day that we're apart, it gets worse. I have to try."

She releases me before we walk outside. I close the door and double check the lock. Driving twelve hours in hopes of talking to Jovie is crazy. But now more than ever, I need her and I know she needs me.

CHAPTER 31

JOVIE

THE SPRING AIR surrounds me as I take in the laughter of the two small girl's running through the small neighborhood park. It's my park. Well, not really, but is across the street from my house. It's the place I always seem to find my way back to. To think. To dream. To sort out all the shit that is my life. I've been here on this bench alone, every single day for the last month. Hours pass before I realize it, but that's a good thing. Because being here is soothing.

Dr. Birch may not have been right about much. Well, maybe she was right about a few things. But the one thing I remember her telling me in our first session was that Brownsboro is my home. Now, after all these months of fighting the truth, I think she may be right.

"Are you okay?" the sound of a familiar male voice puts a smile on my face.

"I'm good, Liam. Really good."

He walks around to the front of the bench before sitting down beside me.

"I've checked on you every day since you've been back. I watch you sit here for hours. Today's the first day I've felt like it would be okay to get out of the car and talk." He smiles before leaning into me with his shoulder.

"So now you're a stalker?" I laugh.

"Well, now that you mention it, I guess I kind of am. But I only stalk you."

I miss him. He always puts a smile on my face.

"You know, you were right. I mean, about Houston and my life. It's worse now than it was before I left here."

"You're dad mentioned a few things that happened while you were away. I think it's harder on him and your mom than you think."

"Now I know they did the best that they could. Neither of them knew how to deal with Piper's death. And then they had me. They were afraid. Afraid that I would be taken away, too. So I've stopped blaming them. I know now that everything they did, they did out of fear and love."

"I'm impressed, Jovie. Sounds like you went away to the big city and became an adult."

"No, Liam, not any adult. I'm still the same me, only without a heart. It's still in Houston, and I don't know if I'll ever get it back." I bring my hands to my face and hang my head.

"I'm here if you need me, always." He wraps his arms around me before squeezing me tight. And it feels great. He always knows how to bring a little sunshine into any shitty situation.

"Thanks for stalking me. I feel much safer sitting here every day knowing I have one of Brownsboro's finest a few feet away."

We both stand. I grab his hands and hold onto them for a few seconds. I want to feel something, anything. But it's not the same. He's not Jack.

"You look super-hot in your uniform. I've never actually been this close to you when you're working." I wink.

"Just imagine how hot I look with it off." He rubs his hands up and down my arms.

Nothing tingly, no electricity, or even warmth in his touch. I wish I felt something. Not that I would jump back in his bed. But the feeling of needing someone's touch is one of the greatest sensations in the entire world.

"Remember, I already know exactly how hot you are out of

uniform."

"Just checking, because if you need me to jog your memory, I'll be glad to strip for you—at my place. In, let's say, about an hour." He smiles before he wraps his hands around my waist. Holding me. Needing me. Wanting me. Three feelings I wish I had for him because nothing would feel better than to be bound to him for the rest of the night, but I can't. It would be wrong to give him expectations that there could be more.

"I can't. I'm sorry."

"He really did a number on you, didn't he?"

"He has my heart. And until he releases it, I'll never be able to be happy with anybody else. Please understand. Because I need you as my friend," I plead.

"I do understand. The offer is always open." He jokes before releasing his hold on me.

"See you around. Remember to call me if you need anything," Liam says as he walks toward the steps.

"See ya, stalker. Thanks for, you know… being you," I say.

He raises his hand for a quick wave and then he's gone.

CHAPTER 32

JACK

"I ALMOST LEFT," I lean in behind her and whisper in her ear, "Seeing you with him stirred up something inside of me. Not sure what. But I didn't like it."

"Why did you stay?" she whispers.

"Because you're mine, and I'm not going home without you." I pull her hair back away from her face and gently run my finger over her cheek.

"Jack, I don't know. Can we even survive this?" she reaches for my hand.

"We can survive anything together. But being apart isn't gonna work for me. I love you, Jovie. So go across the street and get all your stuff. We're going home."

She stands before turning to face me. God—she's so fucking beautiful. Perfect. And if I have to beg, I will drop to my knees and do just that.

"There's so much I need to say. I don't know where to start."

"We have plenty of time for that. Forever," I mumble as I pull her in and nuzzle my face into her neck. "God, I've missed you," I whisper against her skin.

"I love you, Jack."

I pull back from her and look into her eyes. Jovie's eyes.

"Let's go get your stuff. It's a long drive home." I interlock my fingers with hers before pulling her toward the steps.

"He called me, but you knew he would, didn't you?" she asks.

"Yes. He showed up at Stone's the night of Annie's party. He wanted you. The thought of you and him. I knew you would never do it, but my mind wouldn't let it go. But, now. Now, I know why. He wanted you because of her. He's really messed up, Jovie," I mutter.

She stops before we leave the playground and says, "He told me everything about them. And how he blames himself. Jack, he's living like you. Except worse. He said that he was thinking of checking himself into a rehab because he drinks. A lot—every day. I don't know. I feel sorry for him." She places a kiss on my chest.

"I'm not telling you what you can or can't do because for you and me to work, we have to trust each other. But let him be. He has family and friends that'll see he gets help if he wants it. Right now, I just want to focus on us. Rebuilding what we had and moving on with our lives, together."

"Will you do me a favor, Jack?"

"Whatever you want." I place my hands on her cheeks and rest my forehead against hers. "Just say it."

"Tell me about her, about my sister."

Yes, I just agreed to talk to her about Piper. I must be going insane. But, if this is what she needs, then I'll give it to her.

So we stand on the edge of the playground for almost an hour. I tell her everything. How we met, the places we went, our friends. I also told her about the sketch of the tattoo, and I held her while she cried. We left Brownsboro, Georgia that day together. I even drove and she rode beside me in the passenger's seat of my Jeep.

CHAPTER 33

JOVIE

"THANK YOU FOR doing this," I say as we make our way to Piper's gravesite.

It's the first time I've been back since that day almost a year ago. The day I fell apart and ended up in the emergency room.

"You don't have to thank me. I need this as much as you do. She was part of both of our lives," he says as he hands me the flowers to place in the secured vase.

This is hard for me, so I can only imagine how Jack feels. Awkward maybe. I don't know. But we've spent many nights talking about the whole screwed up situation. And it will always be difficult because it is what it is. And nothing will ever change it.

"Piper Evans Blake." I read her name as it's written on the tombstone.

"I never knew her as Piper Blake. She always said her name was Evans, Piper Evans. That's one reason I would have never known the two of you were sisters."

"She never used the name Blake. Her name was Piper Evans. My parents didn't get married until she was four. Evans is my mom's maiden name. I think my mom was so pissed at my dad for not marrying her before Piper was born that she never

172

changed her name. But after she died, my dad said that it was only right for her to be remembered as a Blake. Because that's who she was." A single tear rolls down my cheek as I lean into Jack.

He puts his arm around my waist and holds me close.

"You amaze me. Every single day. You are the strongest person I know." He leans down and kisses the top of my head.

"I love you, Piper. And I promise I will spend more time with you because I'm back in town. My life is here now, and I'm not going anywhere." I smile and look up at Jack. "Oh, and I brought Jack with me. He probably won't say much, but just know he's here. And he loves you, too."

Jack let's go of me and drops to his knees. He bows his head and closes his eyes. He's praying. Or at least, that's what it looks like. Or maybe he's talking to her in private. If he needs to talk to her for his closure, then that's what I want. He has to let go of the guilt. It wasn't his fault. I will never blame him. Never. I want to give him privacy, but I want to hold him. He doesn't need to hurt alone. So I drop to my knees and lean into him. He raises his head and turns to face me. His eyes are glassy.

"Are you okay? I can leave and let you have some time alone with her. Whatever you need, Jack. Just tell me." I gently wrap my hands around his arm.

"No, don't leave. I need you here, beside me."

He helps me stand and then he does the same. And just like that, he seems better. Relaxed. At peace.

I turn toward Piper and continue to talk to her. "Mom and Dad are good. They're not real happy about my living situation." I smile at Jack, "Other than that, everything with them is okay. Oh, I don't know if you know this or not, because I'm not sure what they tell you when they visit, but Mom stopped drinking. You would be so proud of her. She hasn't had a drink since the night, well, since the night you left us. So that's good news. I think we're gonna go for now, but I'll be back. Soon." I place my hand in Jack's before we turn and walk away from the grave. Once we get to the parking lot, he stops and faces me.

"Thank you for bringing me here. I didn't realize how much I needed this. But everything is all right now. We're okay. And I believe she's good with us." His lips touch mine softly. "I love you. So. Damn. Much," he whispers.

I pull back and look up into his brown eyes and remember the very first time I met him. In the bathroom against the door. How badly I wanted him to kiss me that night. But he's made up for it a million times.

"How did I get so lucky?" I smile.

He laughs. "You think what we have is luck?"

I nod before leaning into his chest.

He pushes a strand of hair behind my ear before he says,

"Babe, this isn't luck—it's fate."

The End

NOTE FROM THE AUTHOR

ANXIETY IS REAL. It's no fun for anyone. Most people don't understand what it's like to live in constant fear of when it will attack again. Racing thoughts, worry, and the inability to control your own body. The fear. It's always there. Where will I be when it strikes again? How will I control it? Will I die? Maybe this time it's not anxiety. Maybe this time it really is a heart attack or maybe a stroke. My face is tingling—my left arm is numb. Those are symptoms. Of both. I'm right—I am dying.

Yes. The fear is real. Real damn scary. Everything can be fine one minute and then the next you've lost control. Anxiety does not make you crazy, it only makes you stronger because you have to learn to manage it. And you can—so, if you are one of the thousands of people who suffer from an anxiety disorder—please get help. Talk to your health care provider or a counselor. There are even support groups you can join. Don't suffer in silence because you are embarrassed. Your life is too valuable to continue to live with constant worry over when the next anxiety attack will happen. Know that you are not alone. There are other people just like you. And there are also those who truly want to help you get better. So, please—stop suffering and talk to somebody—get help.

Start with this web site: http://www.adaa.org/finding-help
The Anxiety and Depression Association of America

ACKNOWLEDGMENTS

WOW. WRITING TWISTED FATE has been quite the adventure. One that I did not go on alone. I feel very fortunate to have connected with so many wonderful people on this journey.

Teresa Funke—Even though we didn't finish this project together—it was you who first believed in Jack and Jovie and their story. You taught me to write, to edit, to rewrite, and not to give up. I thank you for your knowledge, support, and encouragement because it was what I needed to see this story through…until the end.

Kristi Falteisek with Sassy Savvy Fabulous—Thank you for everything you do! I realize I probably say this to you almost daily, but it's the truth. There is no way I could have made it through the last two months without your knowledge and expertise. Your patience and ability to guide me through the marketing and promoting part of this journey has been an amazing experience. Again—thank you for everything—you have been wonderful.

Stacey, CeCe, and Radka—My betas. You guys are fabulous. Thank you for telling me what I needed to hear, even if it wasn't what I wanted to hear. And thank you Radka and Stacey for taking bits and pieces of my story at a time—sorry I would leave you hanging until I had time to write more. You guys are awesome!

My editor, Rogena Mitchell-Jones of RMJ Manuscript Service—Thank you for taking on the incredible task of making my writing presentable. It worked—you did an excellent job. And I appreciate you doing all of this without changing my writing style. Thank you! Thank you! You're absolutely brilliant.

To my husband. You are wonderful, but I guess you already knew that, huh? Thanks for putting up with my many hours locked away in my office or talking about this book to the point of making you want to go anywhere just to get away from the sound of my voice. And yes, I have read through it for the last time—for now. But guess what? I've started the next one. So, at least I'll have something new to talk about. Oh—and thank you for reading Jack and Jovie's story—it meant more to me than you'll ever know.

To my son—even though you're grown—well, kind of grown. Thank you for asking about 'my book' with each phone call. It's finally done, so you can stop telling me how many words I have to write every day to finish it before my deadline. You are my absolute greatest accomplishment. And I'm thankful every day that I'm your mom.

To my mom and dad. Thank you for always believing in me and giving me the freedom to make my own decisions. Sometimes, it took me the long way around to get to where I was supposed to be, but I always made it.

Drew Truckle—Thank you for being my Jack. You are one of the kindest people I know and have gone above and beyond what I would have expected in helping me promote Twisted Fate. Thank you again for everything. It truly means so much to me.

Cassy Roop—You Rock! You have mad talent, and I am so excited that you shared it with me on this project. You are not only my cover designer and all around go to person for teasers, branding, website design, etc., but I also consider you a friend. Thanks for chatting with me and walking me through issues that may or may not pertain to graphic design. Thanks so much for everything!

Eric David Battershell—Thank you for the perfect image of Drew for the cover of Twisted Fate. You are so much more than the photographer—always kind and willing help me promote my book—whether a teaser, cover reveal, or release. You have truly been there every step of the way—and I greatly appreciate it!

Alex Maxwell, you are an amazing poet. Thank you for the beautiful poem for my book. It's perfect. But most of all…thanks for being such a great friend.

JM Nash, you are absolutely marvelous! You have walked me through, or should I say, led me out of more crap than I even care to discuss. I'm so very thankful I met you, because not only have you been my sounding board, but also a great friend, always giving me advice about things I know absolutely nothing about. Because, remember, I don't know how to do anything but write, and you, my friend, can do everything—write, graphic design, swag design, size photographs, format, market… Do I need to go on? Thank you for your guidance and friendship.

Terrie Meerschaert with Indie Editing Services—Thank you for last minute proofreading. I appreciate you so much.

A special thank you to Kerry Calloway. You have supported me since the beginning. Thanks for sharing all of my teasers and promoting me every week since that first teaser came out about six months ago. You are truly a remarkable person!

To every blogger, reader, author, and friend who has shared my teasers and cover, or who has promoted my book—thank you—because without your support, no one would know Twisted Fate even existed.

To the readers—thank you for taking a chance on a new author. You guys are the best! I really hope you enjoy Jack and Jovie's story.

CONNECT WITH EMERY

Facebook: www.facebook.com/emeryjacobsauthor
Twitter: @ejacobswrites
Instagram: www.instagram.com/emery_jacobs
Email: emeryjacobswrites@gmail.com

Newsletter Sign up:
http://eepurl.com/bPxj5f

Facebook Reader Group:
https://www.facebook.com/groups/954199601323358/

ABOUT THE AUTHOR

EMERY JACOBS GREW UP in Southern Arkansas and has lived most of her adult life in Northern Louisiana. She spends her days working as a Nurse Practitioner in rural health and her nights reading, writing, and occasionally, sleeping.

She loves real life romance…lots of angst and heartbreak, but always a happy ending.

www.ingramcontent.com/pod-product-compliance
Lightning Source LLC
Chambersburg PA
CBHW061231170626
46809CB00007B/2617